"You say your name is not Serena?"

"No," Tammie said.

"Then how do you explain that picture I showed you?" Dylan asked. He pulled the snapshot out of his pocket and slapped it down on the table in front of her.

The shock Tammie felt the first time she saw the picture hadn't lessened. Her face might not be a perfect match with the woman's in the photo, but they were very similar. "I can't, which is why I agreed to talk to you."

"The man in the picture is my brother."

"I've never seen him before," Tammie said.

Dylan sighed in disbelief. "Okay. Play it that way."

"What do you want from me?" Tammie asked.

"How about the truth?"

Isn't that what she'd come here for? The truth. And yet with each passing moment, the truth seemed to be becoming stranger than fiction.

LISA MONDELLO

Lisa's love of writing romance started early when she penned her first romance novel (a full fifty-eight pages long, but who's counting) at the age of ten. She then went on to write a mystery script that impressed her sixth grade teacher so much he let her and her friends present it as a play to the whole grade. There was no stopping her after that! After going to college for sound recording technology and managing a Boston rock band for four years, she settled down with her husband of over sixteen years and raised a family. Although she's held many jobs through the years, ranging from working with musicians and selling kitchen and catering tools to teaching first and second graders with special needs how to read and write, her love of writing has always stayed in the forefront, and she is now a full-time freelance writer. While she has published seven novels over the past ten years, this is her first book for Steeple Hill Love Inspired Suspense and in many ways it feels like coming home. Lisa lives in western Massachusetts with her husband, four children (who never cease to amaze her as they grow), a very pampered beagle and a rag doll cat who thinks she owns them all.

Cradle of Secrets
LISA MONDELLO

Steeple
Hill®

Published by Steeple Hill Books™

STEEPLE HILL BOOKS

Steeple
Hill®

ISBN-13: 978-0-373-44268-3
ISBN-10:   0-373-44268-8

CRADLE OF SECRETS

Printed in U.S.A.

And you will know the truth,
and the truth will make you free.
—*John* 8:32

I've heard many times that the best part of life is the journey, not the destination, and I thank God that my husband, Tom, my strongest supporter in my writing journey, is still the man I get to journey through life with even after twenty years together.

I am blessed to have a wide net of support around me. Many thanks to my children, Ben, Melyssa, Becky and LeeAnne, for putting up with me and enduring take-out during the writing of this book (I'm not sure that was a huge sacrifice on their part) and my family for all their encouragement.
To Tracy Ritts, Natalie Damschroder, Cathy McDavid and Cathy Andorka for their constant friendship and making this leg of the journey so much fun. You guys are the best!

Special thanks to my agent, Michelle Grajkowski, who continues to believe in me even when I have doubts. And finally, to my editor, Jessica Alvarez, for all her patience and support.

This book is dedicated with love to my grandmother, Bessy Mondello.

ONE

"Take one step closer and I'll shoot!" Tammie Gardner shouted threateningly, putting her hands up like a shield.

Bill stood in her classroom doorway and frowned. "Tammie, we need to talk."

"Later, Professor Lewis," she said, lifting her head only long enough to catch his expression after the formal use of his name, which he hated but she loved to tease him with. "I've just spent the last two hours sorting through all these papers. It's a mess, but it's an organized mess. I don't need you sitting on my desk and tossing things around like you always do."

This being only her second semester at Winchester College, she wasn't used to how hectic the end of the school year was, and time had gotten away from her. With her full class schedule, she was fighting time to get all her grades completed by the end of the semester.

She glanced up. Bill was still frowning. "I need to talk to you, Tammie. This is really important."

She chuckled. "Of course it is. It always is. But can it wait until I get these grades into the book?"

To keep the papers from flying around the room,

Tammie had turned off the fan that normally bathed her face with a somewhat comfortable breeze in the oppressive June heat. This hundred-year-old university building seemed determined to remain hot, and her second-floor classroom felt like a sauna. Without the fan, sweat bubbled on her forehead and upper lip. She wiped it away as she glanced quickly at the door again.

"What are you doing back on campus so early, anyway? I thought you had some urgent, urgent errand to run." Not looking at him, she searched her desk for paperclips. When she found half a box, she started clipping and stacking papers until she could see her desk again.

"Tam, we need to talk," Bill said again. This time, his words came out in a rush. It wasn't like him to ignore her questions. Bill was too predictable to be someplace other than where he said he'd be. Ever since she'd met him in junior-high school, she'd been able to anticipate his every move before he made it.

He was the most levelheaded, even-keeled person she'd ever met—not one to get rattled about anything. But he was still standing at the door, his narrow shoulders slumped slightly, his expression drawn. Her blood ran cold.

Bill was the head of the department—her friend, but also her boss. Had the college decided not to renew her contract? *Lord, please don't let it be more bad news. This job is all that's kept me together this past year.*

"Do you really have to make it this scary, Bill?"

He didn't respond. After a moment of strained silence, save for the janitor whistling "Singing in the Rain" down the hall, Tammy said, "Bill…?"

It was then that she spotted the thick white envelope in

Bill's hand. Somehow, she hadn't noticed it when he'd walked into the room.

He heaved a heavy sigh. "You're going to need to sit down for this."

She did, her heart hammering against her ribs, and the air in the room feeling like a vacuum squeezing the breath from her lungs.

A few quick strides across the room, and Bill handed her the envelope. She glanced at it, puzzled. The return address was that of the laboratory they'd sent their samples to, as part of their class DNA project. All the students had taken samples from a parent or sibling and matched it with their own DNA to show the genetic makeup of their families. Bill and Tammie had participated in the study with their students.

At first, it had been painful for Tammie. As an only child, she could only match her DNA against her parents'. But they'd been killed nearly two years before, so she'd used hair from a treasured brush set her mother had always kept on her dressing table. Tears welled up in her eyes again, just as they had that day, when she'd carefully plucked the thin blond strands from the bristles and placed them in a plastic bag. It had been the same when she scraped small shavings from her father's old razor.

She sighed, placing a hand over her rapidly beating heart, then laughed nervously. "Is this what you're all riled up about? I thought you were going to tell me I was fired."

"Tammie, wait—"

"I was getting worried we wouldn't have the results of the study before the end of the semester. I would have had to completely restructure the final exam."

Bill swallowed and shook his head. It was barely perceptible, but that small movement brought the dread she'd felt earlier rushing back.

She slapped the envelope on her cluttered desk, bringing both hands up to her face. "Oh, don't tell me they messed up the test. They didn't lose someone's sample, did they?"

Bill reached across the desk to where Tammie had dropped the envelope, opened it and pulled out a small piece of paper.

"These results came in a week ago. But I had to make sure they were correct before I showed them to you."

Irritation stirred inside her. "A week? Bill, the entire class project hinges on these results. You know that. I've had to be very creative these last few days, thinking up ways the students could work around the results, and all this time you already had them? Why did you keep this from me?"

"Just…sit down, Tammie. You need to read your report."

"Mine? Why mine?"

Her eyes went to his, then down to the page he'd handed her.

There were no names on the page, only numbers. She'd done that to protect the privacy of her students when the results were examined by the class. Since she'd personally numbered the samples for both classes, she knew which results belonged to each student, and she'd shared that list with Bill. She scanned the graph and then read the report associated with the data for her sample. Her breath caught in her throat, and her knees buckled.

"No! This has to be some kind of sick joke!"

Easing back against the hard cushion of her desk chair, she forced herself to breathe. In and out. In and out. It didn't help. The room was spinning.

"Bill?" she said, pleading with him. "This has to be a mistake!"

He looked down at her with sympathetic pale blue eyes. "I know this is a blow—"

"Are you kidding me?" she snapped, crumpling the paper in her hand as she fisted her palm. "A blow is when you've got your heart set on getting a promotion and they pass you over for someone else with half your experience. A blow is when you've planned a trip to a five-star hotel in Bali only to end up in a cockroach-infested dive with no running water. This paper is saying my whole life is a lie. That isn't a blow, Bill, it's…it's insanity!"

She stared at her friend, searching for some sign that he was teasing her. She'd forgive him if he were. But the spindly man she'd become close to had never been good at jokes. Oh, he tried to make her laugh, but it always fell flat.

But he was a good listener. And he was her friend. That was what had drawn them together when they met in junior high, and why she'd taken this teaching position a year ago.

After her parents were killed, in a Labor Day boating accident nearly two years ago, she'd shut herself off from the world. If she hadn't been late getting to the marina, she would have died, as well.

For a brief time, she'd even turned away from the Lord, grieving and angry that He'd taken the most precious people in her life and spared her. But she'd soon learned that having the Lord in her heart could help ease her pain.

Bill had methodically pulled her back into the land of the living, convincing her to come back to Winchester, and even pulling some strings to get her a job at the college. Tammie had never felt any great desire to make their

friendship into something romantic, although she suspected Bill had other ideas. The fact that he didn't share
her strong belief in God was a barrier she couldn't cross.

They'd talk for hours, mostly about her parents and her
suspicions that their accident was anything but. Even
though the local investigators were still looking into the
possibility that the boat's engine had been tampered with,
Bill wouldn't let her dwell on it, reminding her that finding
the truth, either way, wouldn't bring her parents back.

Then, one rainy day, she'd closed the door on her grief.
Bill had been the one to pull her out of the pain of loss and
convince her to let the past go. Although it had taken some
doing, he'd convinced Tammie that her suspicions were
merely a figment of her imagination; holding on to them
was only keeping her grief alive. She'd begun attending
church again, finding solace in the teachings of God's grace
that her parents had instilled in her from childhood. But the
suspicion that her parents had been murdered lingered.

"Don't you think I wish it were wrong, Tammie?" Bill
said, his eyes filling as he dropped the folder that defended
all the untruths about her life on the desk in front of her.
"It took you so long to move on after your parents died."

She looked at him sharply. "Don't you mean to get over
the idea that they were murdered?"

"You're a totally different woman than you were then."

"Yeah. And this report says that, doesn't it? How could
you not tell me this? How could you have held on to this
report for a whole week and not said a word?"

"I had to be sure."

Her eyes rested on the torn seal of the white paper. She
didn't want to look at the contents of the envelope but as

if they had a will of their own, her hands were snatching up the thick white envelope and spilling the contents all over her already cluttered desk.

"They're wrong sometimes, right?" *Oh, please, Lord, they have to be wrong this time. Don't take what I have left of them away from me,* Tammie prayed silently.

Bill perched on the edge of her desk, pushing papers around like he always did. His gray tweed blazer gaped open, revealing a black turtleneck. She knew without a doubt that he had a pocket planner tucked in the inside pocket, and a red pen for marking papers. He'd had a banana for breakfast with a cup of black coffee, and for lunch, the tuna sandwich he always stashed away in the right-hand drawer of his desk, along with a Snickers bar and a can of no-name cola. Like always.

She'd needed that kind of predictability after she'd arrived in Winchester, Oregon. She'd tried to get through her grief in her little apartment in Vancouver, Washington, trying to make some sense of her parents' deaths. But it had been no use. Instead of drowning in questions, she'd packed up her Volkswagen Bug and moved to the town her parents had lived in when she was a young child and gotten a job at the local college.

Bill had been her rock then. But the contents of one seemingly innocent white envelope were making the very foundation of her life crumble beneath her again.

Tammie closed her eyes and said a silent prayer as she gulped back tears. When she was done, she unfolded the report and clamped her top teeth down on her trembling bottom lip. She kept at it until she felt the pain. The smell of glue from the envelope tickled her nose. With shaking hands she couldn't control, she found the report for her sample and read the words that severed the last remaining thread to a life she had once owned.

The DNA results show less than one tenth of one percent chance that sample 0017 and 0022 are biologically related..."

She read the words repeatedly, not wanting to believe them, letting her tears spill freely down her cold cheeks. After checking the second sample she'd used for her father, she choked on a sob, burying her face in her hands and allowing the papers to drift to her desk.

"This is impossible..." she whispered.

"I'm so sorry, Tammie," Bill said on a heavy sigh. "I'd give anything if it weren't true. I made them check the samples to make sure they weren't contaminated in any way. They weren't."

They weren't her parents. Who were they? Who was she? They'd never said a word.

"They were all I had, and now I find out they weren't even mine."

How could that be? How could she have lived her entire life not knowing that the man and woman who raised her as their own were not her biological parents?

"Yes, they were, Tammie. In every way that counts, they were your parents." Bill started to take her hand in his, but she pushed it away.

"I wasn't supposed to even take this test. It was all for a stupid class project. My sample was only there to round out the results. If I hadn't done this, I never would have known..."

"This doesn't change anything."

She glared at Bill. "Maybe not for you. Your life is

exactly the same as it was when you woke up this morning, when you walked into my office ten minutes ago. I have no idea who I really am or where I came from. My whole life has been a lie."

She snatched the last tissue out of the box on her desk and blew her nose. "How did this happen? How could my parents have kept something so vitally important from me my whole life? Why didn't they tell me?"

"Maybe they didn't know, Tammie."

"What? You mean like being switched at birth?"

"It happens. Hospitals get busy, and some baby gets put in the wrong bassinet or the wristbands get switched. It happens."

Tammie stared off into the far corner of her office. It always amazed her how life could turn upside down in a matter of seconds.

"Yeah, it happens. But don't you think by now someone would have found out? I mean, I've had blood drawn tons of times. Don't you think someone would have questioned my blood type if it didn't match my parents? Nothing got past my mother. She was so good at keeping records. Nothing like me." She closed her eyes, then whispered, "Nothing like me."

Sighing, she glanced down at the report. "This test doesn't show blood type."

"Maybe you have the same blood type as one of your parents. Lots of people share the same blood type." He shrugged. "Okay, so you weren't switched at birth. Maybe you *were* adopted."

"If I was adopted, why didn't they tell me? They never kept anything from me."

"How do you know?"

"Because I know." She stared at the envelope and sniffed. "Maybe they just didn't want me to find out."

"Don't go there again, Tam. I beg you. It won't bring your parents back."

Her shoulders sagged. "Why don't you believe me about this? I knew my parents. If I so much as had a hangnail, they took me to the doctor's office. If they really *didn't* know I wasn't their biological daughter, they would have found out. I don't think this was a mistake, Bill," she said, trying to keep her pain out of her voice. "They knew. They just chose not to tell me. The question is, *why?*"

The sting was so sharp, it was like losing them all over again. The one thing she'd learned since her parents' deaths was that life couldn't go on unless you picked yourself up and put your best foot forward. The first step was admitting the truth of what was in that file.

"Okay. Let's say you *were* adopted. Not every parent reveals something like that to their kid. They might have been afraid you would reject them. It doesn't have to be something sinister."

"I loved my parents. I would never reject them no matter what this file has to say." She lifted the paper, then let it slide to the far side of her desk.

Bill came around to her side. "You can't ask them about it. Just let it go."

Tammie swiped another tear and stared up at his pleading eyes. "You of all people know I can't do that. They were the most open, honest people I knew. It doesn't make sense that they would have kept this from me."

She looked at Bill and, through tear-filled eyes, said the things she couldn't put into words.

Bill sighed. "You're not returning to the college next year, are you?"

Her bottom lip wobbled. "I've always suspected their deaths weren't an accident. A diesel boat doesn't explode when taking on fuel unless something ignites it. Even a faulty wire would have caused only a small fire, giving them plenty of time to get off the boat. I saw the explosion from the parking lot. The boat went up like an atomic bomb. Even the fire investigator said they should have had time to escape, and yet the boat was engulfed almost immediately.

"Things just don't add up. They were acting so weird, insisting I go away with them before school was over. I would have been on that boat, too, if I hadn't been so late getting there. I need to know the truth. But I honestly have no idea where to start."

"You should start here."

Dylan peered over the side of the flatbed truck. Mrs. Burdett stood at the side of the road, giving him instructions on how to retie the ropes that were supposed to keep her priceless antiques in place. This not being the first time he'd been given a lesson from the elderly woman, he'd actually thought of passing by her when he saw her truck pulled over to the side of the road.

But guilt crept up his spine, reminding him he was not only a cop, but a Marine, as well. Or at least he used to be. And at one time, he'd even been a Boy Scout. That still meant extending help to little old ladies in need, even when he was practically being forced out of town against his will.

"Nah, you need more support on this end."

He wrapped the thin, almost clothesline-like rope around the solid sideboard snug up against the back of the truck. Even as he did it, he knew the rope was going to snap again.

"Who packed the truck for you, Mrs. Burdett?" he called down.

"Trudie," she said, reminding him of her request that he call her by her first name. Tipping her frayed straw hat up so that she could meet his gaze, she harrumphed.

His look was apologetic. "Okay, Trudie."

"Had to do it myself. That no good, lazy-boned grandson of mine wasn't around. Probably down at Handies again with his good-for-nothing girlfriend. Seems all they do these days is play pool, the two of them. I told him I had to get these pieces down to Jackson's. They have to be photographed for the catalogs before the end of the day, or I'll miss my spot during the auction. And I've held that spot going on thirty-three years now."

"Well, I'd hate for you to lose your spot. But we're going to need something a little stronger than what you have here to secure these pieces, or you'll lose the entire truckload down Main Street before you even make it to Jackson's."

Dylan jumped down from the truck and stood directly in front of the elderly woman. She was no more able to haul this furniture onto a truck by herself than a toddler. He had a feeling he wasn't the first Boy Scout to have helped her out today.

"You shouldn't be moving furniture anymore. You don't want to break your hip again, do you?"

She straightened her spine. "Who's been telling you such things? Betcha it's that new waitress down at the diner. She can't keep her mouth shut for breathing. But don't you worry. There's nothing wrong with my bones, son. I got my new hip two years ago, and I'm as good as I was the day I started the Auction Acres."

Dylan winked. "Course you are. And just as pretty, too."

Her quick grin twisted into a forced frown, but Dylan knew she'd been flattered by the compliment, as transparent as it was.

"Don't you go sweet-talking *this* woman. If you were this slick with the young ones you'd be married off by now, not chasing down that brother of yours."

Dylan winced at the mention of Cash, but he let it pass. He'd already grilled Trudie once about him, and it had been clear she didn't have a clue who he was talking about. The one person who did, Serena Davco, was the one he hadn't been able to see.

"Next time, you might want to think of calling some professionals to help out, if Maynard is too busy," he said, changing the subject. "All it would have taken is one more pothole and you'd have lost the whole load, instead of just that chair."

He pointed to the side of the road, where what was left of a wooden chair sat broken and splintered. "Doesn't bode well for business."

"No, it does not. I'll be sure to tell Maynard that bit of news." She harrumphed again, this time with a little additional steam. "Not that it'll do an ounce of good for the half ounce of sense he has in his head these days."

Trudie was still grumbling about her kin as she climbed into the truck, pulled out onto the road and sped off, the engine coughing black fumes that mixed with the kicked-up dirt. Laughing, Dylan strode back to his Jeep and swung the door open. Before he could climb in, a red subcompact car with rental plates rolled to a stop in front of him.

Dylan did a double take; he couldn't believe his eyes. Looking up at the sky he thought, *God, there may not be a place for me to lay my head in this town, but I knew You wouldn't let me down before I had to leave. Thanks for the help.* Maybe he wouldn't be leaving town just yet.

Heat seared his cheeks as the woman behind the wheel of the car rolled down her window. Reaching into the Jeep, he grabbed the picture he'd found in his brother's apartment and took a quick glance back at the woman just to make sure. He really didn't need the extra look. He'd memorized the face in the picture over the two months since Cash had gone AWOL. This was the woman. *Serena Davco.* Since the photo had been taken, her hair had been cut in a straight style that fell around her cheeks, but the color was the same, as were the dark blue eyes.

The woman's smile was pleasant as she cocked her head to one side. "Hi. I was hoping you could help me out. I'm looking for a hotel in town that might have some vacancies. Do you know of any? Every place I've tried is full."

Dylan tossed the picture onto the driver's seat and strode into the middle of the road. He'd been knocking on Serena Davco's door for the better part of a month, and he'd had the maid and the housekeeper slam the door in his face each time. There was no way he was letting her get away with not talking to him now. It was long past the time for patience and small talk.

"Well, it's about time you showed your face, lady. Where on earth is my brother?"

TWO

The woman blinked at his hostility. Normally Dylan wouldn't have been so harsh with a stranger, but he'd been trying unsuccessfully to get a meeting with Serena Davco the entire time he'd been in the small Massachusetts town of Eastmeadow. If demanding answers in the middle of the one street running through the center of town was the only chance he had to get information, then so be it. He was beyond ready to get down to business.

"Excuse me?"

"It's not that hard a question. My brother. Where did he go?"

She blinked again, her mouth agape. "I'm sorry. I don't have a clue what you're talking about."

Anger like hot coals surged through him and he laughed. He'd already spent too much time in this hick town getting the runaround from everyone he talked to. But Cash had been clear about one thing. And Serena Davco was it.

"Oh, really? Cash started talking all crazy about coming here to rescue you, because you were in danger. That was nearly three months ago." Dylan threw up his hands, then let them fall to his sides as he glanced at the open meadows on both sides of the road that gave the town its name. "Well, here you are. You don't look like you're in danger from anything but a stray cow, but no one has heard from my brother in over two months."

"I'm just trying to find a hotel to stay in while I'm in town."

A fingernail of irritation raked up Dylan's spine, sending what little patience he had left blowing out the top of his head. He raked his hand over his head just to make sure it was still there.

"Now this is a twist. Lady, you live in the biggest mansion this side of the Mississippi. That house on the hill is practically a hotel all by itself."

The woman quickly rolled up her window and started to put the car into drive.

"Hey, wait, wait—you're not going anywhere." Before he knew what he was doing, his hand was inside the window, trying to keep the glass from closing. But she was quicker than him, and the window shut, squeezing his palm.

Desperate to keep his only lead from vanishing, Dylan pulled his hand out and ran in front of the car, effectively stopping her escape. That is, unless she was inclined to run him over. At that point, he didn't care. His brother had walked into something dangerous and was now missing. This woman was the reason for it. He wasn't letting her get away without finding out what happened to Cash.

Tammie stared in total disbelief at the crazy man glaring back at her from beyond her windshield. *This guy's a lunatic! What have I gotten myself into?*

"Oh, God, please help me out of this one." As she contemplated her next move, she continued with a silent prayer her father had taught her as a child. *The Lord is my strength and my shield. My heart trusts in Him, and I am helped. My heart leaps for joy, and I will praise Him in song.*

The thing she hated most about these economy rental cars—besides the artificial fresh smell—was that they had four-cylinder engines with no pickup. She usually wasn't a person who felt the need to go from zero to seventy in two seconds flat, but now would be a good opportunity to test what this engine could handle.

Giving herself a moment to decide whether she wanted to tick this madman off any more than he was, she leaned on the horn.

It didn't seem to faze him at all. He just placed his wide palms on the hood of the car and continued to glower at her. She saw his dark blue eyes narrow as a gust of wind blew the curls of his chocolate-brown hair up and into his face. His black T-shirt did little to hide the muscles underneath.

"I'm not going anywhere."

"Well, *I* am," she called back. Inside the car, with the windows rolled up, her voice sounded loud. Her fingers white-knuckled the steering wheel as she licked her lips, contemplating her escape.

Dear God, help me get out of this one. And if You can manage a little bit of speed, that'd be great, too.

"Where is Cash? What did you do to him?"

Tammie shook her head, her eyes darting from one side of the road to the other in search of someone who might bear witness. She'd seen a truck filled with furniture pass by before she stopped, but it was long gone. The only souls around were cows and a few horses grazing in a field, seemingly unconcerned with the disturbance in the street.

She braved a glance in her rearview mirror. "The Lord

helps those who help themselves." Punching the transmission into reverse, she hit the gas and the car sped backward, the tires leaving tread on the road. As she gained speed, she cut the wheel and did a 180-degree turn. Heart pounding, Tammie glanced once again in her rearview mirror to see the psychotic man waving his arms at her.

Even when the man was out of sight, her pulse kept pounding. With the back of her hand, she wiped the sweat from her forehead. Though it was June, the temperature outside had shot up well into the eighties and with the window rolled up, it hadn't taken long for the inside of the car to get hot.

She'd passed a small, run-down-looking efficiency motel on the edge of town, but she still opted to go deeper into Eastmeadow, in hopes of a nicer place to stay in the center of town. But if the local folk were anything like this guy, she was better off in a dive she could escape to if need be. As long as it had a kitchenette where she could brew some coffee, who cared?

Her heart had slowed only marginally when she pulled into the parking lot. There were only a few cars, but the sign said there were no vacancies.

Heaving a sigh, she said to herself, "When did that happen?" Tammie couldn't recall the sign being there earlier, when she'd driven past it. But then, she'd quickly dismissed the idea of staying here, so she'd probably just overlooked it the first time.

Undaunted, she pulled into a parking space. Killing the engine, she reasoned that at least the motel clerk would know of other places in the area she could stay, which was more than she knew now. A town as quaint as Eastmeadow probably had a few bed-and-breakfasts that were worth checking out. She preferred something comfortable and homey to being locked up in a small room.

As she walked up the cracked concrete path to the side door, she began to think that perhaps Bill had been right. Maybe all she was doing by coming here was chasing something that couldn't bring her happiness. Couldn't bring her parents back.

Lord, I know better than to question You for taking them from me. But why didn't they tell me the truth? I need to know why. And if coming here doesn't bring the answers, please help me find peace in that.

She'd fought that battle nearly two years ago, after her parents' deaths. She'd been angry, and she'd blamed the Lord for taking her only family from her. She knew better now. God was merciful, and whatever plan He had for her and her parents was not for her to question. She wasn't questioning the Lord anymore. She was questioning her parents.

The cool air in the foyer bathed her face as she stepped inside. An older man sat behind the counter reading a newspaper. The small color TV at the end of the counter was tuned to a sports channel, but he didn't seem to be paying attention. At her approach, the man dipped the newspaper only slightly, so that she could see his face fully, and he quickly nodded toward the front window.

"Sign says no vacancies," he grunted, then stuck his nose back in the paper without so much as a glance in her direction.

"I saw the sign," she said, pointing outside the window. "I thought maybe you knew of another hotel in town or even a bed-and-breakfast that might have a room."

"You must not be from around here," he said, just his gaze rising to meet her face. Then he slowly dropped the paper and laid it on the counter.

"Hey, aren't you…?" He stared for a moment, as if he were waiting for her to say something.

"Ah… I just got into town this morning."

The clerk nodded. "There aren't any vacancies anywhere in the area, with the auction coming up this week. Most reservations are booked as early as the year before. I had to kick two people out of the motel just this morning to make room for guests who'd booked last year."

Tammie forced herself to keep her disappointment from showing.

"You in town for the auctions?"

"Ah, yeah, I thought I'd check it out." She didn't know anything about any auction, but any information she could get about the town would help her decide where to start asking questions.

He laughed, placing his hand on top of the paper. "Little lady, this isn't a place people just wander into during auction week. This small town of three thousand is going to grow to about a hundred thousand, and stay that way until the auctions are over. People come from all over the country to this event. In a matter of days, this place is going to be crawling with people. The traffic on these roads will be horrendous, and only the locals know how to navigate their way around it."

The clerk pulled a map out of a container filled with pamphlets from area businesses and started circling spots in town. Motioning her closer to the counter, he stuck his finger on a map. "Now, here's Jackson's—they're the biggest auction house, but they don't open until three days into the week. Auction Acres is the first on the row, but these days Trudie Burdett is showing her goods with Jackson's. She gets better exposure that way. Then these open fields are vendors in tents. Those fields go for about a half mile on both sides of the road. They've got everything from furniture to jewelry to antique lunch boxes for sale."

Tammie viewed the map with amazement. "Wow. This is huge."

The elderly clerk laughed and thrust the paper out to her. "No one ever gets through the whole thing in a day. It's best to plan ahead. Make sure you take this map with you."

"But what about hotels?" Tammie asked.

The man shrugged. "If you don't have a reservation locked in somewhere within a twenty-mile radius, I'm afraid you're out of luck. About the only place around here with room is the campground. You might be able to rent a trailer there, if they aren't all spoken for by now. Julius usually has a few on loan for people like yourself."

Tammie stifled a sigh, refusing to allow herself to be discouraged. Twenty miles wasn't all that far to drive, if it meant getting information about her parents.

The letter she'd found in her mother's hatbox from someone named Dutch was the only thing she had to go on. It was dated a few months after she was born. The little scribbled note simply read that Dutch had taken care of everything—not to worry and to stay safe. What that meant, Tammie didn't know. She had never heard her parents mention a person named Dutch. But that was the only thing she had to go on here in Eastmeadow.

She'd avoided looking at the hatbox and its contents

after her parents died. But when she discovered she wasn't their biological daughter, she'd gone looking for something that could prove the DNA evidence wrong. That small piece of mail with an Eastmeadow, Massachusetts, postmark had made her cross the country in search of answers.

"Thank you for your help," she said, turning toward the door.

"Good luck finding a place to stay. And hang on to your wallet."

His comment made her stop and turn back. "Why is that?"

"If the fever for some good antiques don't make you spend your life savings, thieves of another kind will take it from you. We get a lot of vagrants in town during auction week, trying to score, if you know what I mean. An event like this doesn't always bring out the cream of the crop."

She smiled. "Thanks for the warning."

The hot June air hit her in the face as she walked out the door, but she refused to feel defeated. Twenty miles to the nearest hotel? Not a big deal, but if traffic was anything like the clerk said, she'd be spending her whole day in the car, instead of talking to people who might actually be able to lead her to this Dutch. And with so many people from out of town flooding the streets, who could she talk to who would have any information that could help her?

With the key chain still in her hand, she punched the unlock button and watched the lights flash on her rental car. She didn't notice the Jeep that had pulled in next to her—or the man who'd jumped out—until he was standing by her side.

Jumping back against her car, she stared into the eyes

of the maniac from down the road. His face wasn't nearly as menacing as it had been earlier. She glanced at the motel window. The clerk had his nose stuck in the paper again, but she was sure that if she screamed, he'd hear her.

Making her voice steady, she said, "Go away."

"I need to talk with you."

"Good for you. I don't need to talk with you." Tammie gripped the handle behind her and pulled the car door open, but the man pushed it shut, then took a step back and leaned against it.

"Look, I know I frightened you back there, and I'm really sorry. It seems I left my manners back in Chicago. But I really need to talk with you about my brother. I've been in this stinking town for a month, and I've gotten nowhere."

This was what the clerk was warning her about.

"I'm sorry to hear that. But I have my own problems." She'd meant to be droll, to let him think he hadn't really scared her earlier and wasn't frightening her now. But her words fell flat.

"I suppose I deserve that. But, please, just a few minutes."

"I'm busy."

The man rolled his eyes. "I know, I know, you're looking for a hotel. I'm sure the clerk told you the same thing he told me this morning as I was tossed out of my room."

"You have a way with people, don't you?"

"The room was already booked," he insisted impatiently. "And there aren't any other vacant rooms within miles. I'm sure the manager told you that, too. If you insist on finding a room outside of town, instead of staying in your own house, I'll be happy to help you. But before we do that, just answer a few questions about Cash."

Frustration wound its way through her. "I've never met anyone named Cash. Now, if you'll excuse me…"

He pointed across the street to a small diner that doubled as a convenience store. "I'll buy you a cup of coffee or hot chocolate or iced tea. All I'm asking for is ten minutes of your time, and then I'll be out of your hair."

"I told you, I can't help you. I have no idea who or what you're talking about." She yanked at the car door again, but the man pressed his back against it, keeping her from opening it completely.

"You say you don't know Cash. Then how do you explain this?"

He thrust a small picture in front of her, and her blood went cold. The color snapshot had been taken during the winter months. Two people were standing knee-deep in snow, a man wearing a dark green parka, a woman in a cream fur-lined one. She didn't recognize the man in the picture, only that he bore a resemblance to this man who seemed determined to harass her.

But the face of the woman made her swallow hard. It was like looking in a mirror.

"Ten minutes," the man pleaded softly. "That's all I'm asking."

Tammie's stomach growled. After her red-eye flight from the West Coast and the hassle of getting a rental car and finding her way out to Eastmeadow, her body had already burned off the energy from the coffee and donut she'd picked up before renting her car.

Her plan this morning had been to find a hotel in town and sleep the day away to recover from jet lag. She hadn't counted on a flight delay, a long line at the rental counter and difficulty in getting a room. If she was going to drive even another half hour to find a place to stay, she was going to need to refuel.

Lord, I have to be mighty tired to be considering a cup of coffee with a crazy man.

There were cars in the parking lot of the diner across the street. That meant people. Safety was already an issue, it seemed, and this guy hadn't proven his intentions were honorable. And there was a good chance that, whatever move she made, he was just going to follow her anyway.

She shut the car door. She wouldn't let him know that seeing the picture had rattled her even more than that episode on the road. He said he had questions, and now she had a string of her own.

"I'm walking across to the diner to get a cup of coffee for myself, and if you happen to walk with me, then I'll listen. But that's all. If you start badgering me again, or make any threats, I'm calling the police."

His lips lifted into a smile. "Then I'm your man. I've spent the last six months on the force in Chicago."

"Just six months?"

"No, actually, I spent two years on the police force right out of college. I spent twelve years in the United States Marine Corps, until a little less than a year ago. It felt right to go back to the force after that."

Why do I get the feeling I should run? "A Marine, huh?"

He smirked. "I assure you, you're safe with me."

"So you say."

Tammie started across the parking lot toward the road in silence.

So, the crazy man was really a cop from the streets of

Chicago. And a Marine, to boot. *Go figure.* Well, there was safety in numbers, and if the crazy guy tried anything, she'd be in a diner full of people. Her chances were certainly better there than out here on the street.

Tammie glanced at him a few times out of the corner of her eye. He had to be more than ten years older than her twenty-seven years. He was much taller than her, probably over six foot two. His demeanor had changed considerably. The angry man she'd seen in the middle of the road now seemed to have the manners of a gentleman. He put a protective hand out when, in her fatigue, she tried to step too quickly into the road and didn't see the oncoming traffic, and then he opened the door to the diner for her.

"You're dead on your feet, lady," he said.

He didn't have to tell her that. She felt like roadkill, and probably looked like it, too.

"Why don't you have a seat while we wait for the coffee?"

The man pulled out a chair from a table that still had wet streaks on it from being washed. He motioned to the waitress, asking for his usual, plus an extra coffee. The waitress gave him a quick smile, as if he were a regular.

While she waited, Tammie rubbed her burning eyes. Fatigue was winning over her.

"You look like you haven't slept in days. Why are you so exhausted?" the man said, lacing his fingers together.

"I don't sleep very well on planes, and I pulled an all-nighter from the West Coast."

He lifted an eyebrow. "West? What part?"

"Oregon."

He nodded as the waitress set their coffees on the table

with a small stainless steel pitcher of cream and a toasted bagel that smelled wonderful. Her stomach grumbled again.

"I don't even know your name," she said.

"Dylan Montgomery."

He slathered the bagel with cream cheese and placed half of it in front of her on a napkin.

Glancing down at the bagel, she said, "You're trying to butter me up with food, Dylan."

"Is it working?"

She smirked. "Could be. I have a soft spot for bagels and cream cheese. The question is why you're doing it."

His face showed genuine remorse. "I'm sorry I scared you back there. I know better than to approach a woman like a Neanderthal, especially in anger. It was wrong of me."

"Why did you?"

He took a bite of his food and swallowed, seemingly weighing his words. "I'm a little tired myself. Not that that's an excuse for my behavior, just an explanation. You're the last person I know who had any contact with my brother, Serena, and I've been trying to see—"

"Serena?" She frowned. "Who's Serena?"

With the coffee cup at his lips, he said, "Serena Davco. That *is* your name, isn't it?"

"My name is Tammie Gardner."

Dylan paused a second, midbite, and then swallowed. "Tammie Gardner."

He didn't seem convinced, and she didn't care.

"From Oregon?"

"I grew up in Winchester."

He motioned toward the uneaten bagel in front of her. "You should eat."

As she played with the crisp corner of the toasted bagel, Dylan wiped his mouth with a napkin and sat back in his seat. "Do you ever feel like you're in some weird science fiction movie where reality shifts every five minutes?"

Tammie shook her head and lifted a torn piece of the bagel, then popped it in her mouth.

Dylan shrugged. "This town will do that to you."

"Meaning?"

"You say your name is not Serena."

"No."

"Then how do you explain that picture I showed you?"

He pulled the snapshot out of his pocket again and slapped it down on the table. The shock Tammie had felt the first time she saw the picture hadn't lessened. The faces might not be a perfect match, but they were very close.

She picked up the photo and stared. "I can't, which is why I agreed to talk to you."

"The man in the picture is my brother, Cash."

"I've never seen him before."

Dylan sighed in disbelief. "Okay. Play it that way."

"What do you want from me?"

"How about the truth? Cash came here to find Serena Davco—to 'save' her." Dylan waved his hands around as if he thought his brother was a little nuts even to have the idea. Kind of like Tammie had thought Dylan was back in the street. "And here you are, with a face that matches this picture. Except you say your name is not Serena Davco."

She drew in a deep breath, her appetite suddenly gone. Her parents had lived here at one time, and yet they'd never mentioned Eastmeadow to her. There was a woman walking around with her face. She closed her eyes, not wanting to think about the possibility that her parents had known this Serena Davco.

"It's not exactly the same. Our faces, I mean. Maybe you can't see it, but our faces are different."

Dylan leaned forward, his voice low. "Look, Cash said you were in trouble. I'm a police officer. If something has happened and you're in fear for your life, I can help you get protection, from the state police. But I can't if you're not straight with me. And I can't help my brother unless I know the truth about what's going on."

Wasn't that what she'd come here for? The truth? And yet, with each passing moment, the truth seemed to become stranger and stranger.

Tammie looked down at the picture. "I came here looking for the truth, too."

His lips tilted into a slight grin that she found striking. He was a handsome man, with strong features and a rugged look that was alluring.

Dylan nodded. "Good. Progress."

"I think I need to find this Serena Davco and talk to her."

"Well, join the club. It's taken me a month to get *this* far."

"You mean you've never met her?"

Dylan lifted his coffee to his lips and paused to stare at this strange woman. He could see what Cash had seen in her. She was much prettier in person, with eyes that seem to light up a room. That wasn't something you'd get from a snapshot.

But she was playing with him, and he didn't like it. He'd spent the last month trying to talk with this woman, and now that he was face-to-face with her, he was getting the runaround. But Dylan could out-game anyone.

She said her name was Tammie Gardner. He'd have to have his old partner in Chicago, Matt, check that name out later to find out just who Tammie Gardner was and what, if anything, she had to do with Cash. Maybe Tammie Gardner was an alias. If so, he'd find out.

"No, I've never met Serena Davco," he said evenly, then took a sip of his coffee.

She sighed, seeming frustrated.

If she was determined to play this game, then he'd play along with her, earn her trust. Cash wasn't a man to just go off blindly chasing a pretty face. He'd been secretive about his relationship with Serena, and maybe that was a game they'd both played.

It hurt Dylan more than he wanted to admit that his brother hadn't confided in him about something so important until the very end. Until it was too late. He could have helped, if only he'd known.

Maybe this woman had her reasons for not wanting to confess to being Serena Davco in public. Dylan wanted to learn all about those reasons, because he was sure they were at the root of his brother's disappearance.

She put the picture down. "When was this taken?"

"I don't know. But it was the only one I found in my brother's place after he vanished."

"Vanished? You haven't heard from him at all?"

"No. It's been over two months, and that's not like him. He's always been very close to me and our sister."

Dylan squashed the guilt that had been eating at him ever since he made the decision to leave the Marines and come back stateside. He'd been ready to re-enlist after a twelve-year span in the military that had been exciting and rewarding.

But then his kid sister Sonia had phoned him in Indonesia to tell him Cash was acting strange and he should think about not re-enlisting. She'd said it'd be better for him to come back to the States. *For good.*

He'd ripped up his re-enlistment papers and submitted new paperwork to retire permanently from the Marines. As difficult as it was to leave what he loved doing, he hadn't looked back. His family needed him.

Tammie nodded, nibbled on her bottom lip. "I think it's time to go to this mansion where you say Serena Davco lives and check things out. Do you know where it is?"

He tossed a ten on top of the check the waitress had left in front of him. "Follow me."

Less than fifteen minutes later, they pulled up in front of 322 Riverview Road. Dylan had kept a close watch on the car as it drove behind him, making sure Serena didn't try to ditch him by turning down one of the many winding country roads in these parts. He'd been caught on a few by accident these last few weeks.

With a quick breath, he pushed the car door open and climbed outside. She was still sitting in her car, just staring at the mansion, which must have been grand at one time, but now looked like something out of a gothic movie. The brick walkway leading to the front steps was starting to crumble and was covered with moss. Although the flowers were well tended to and the shrubs were trimmed, the wooden gate and the siding on the main dwelling were in serious need of a can of paint.

The flash of fear on Tammie's face as she came up beside him didn't make his resolve waiver. The key to finding his brother was getting this woman to talk to him about their relationship. This woman who claimed her name was Tammie Gardner.

Well, maybe today it was. There had been some rumblings at the diner about mental health issues when he pushed for information about Serena Davco. He'd play the game a little while longer, earn her trust and then he'd get the answers he needed. Maybe being in her own surroundings would make her feel more comfortable.

With a hand placed gently on her back, he walked with her over the brick pathway. At times, it felt as if he was even pushing her toward the front door.

She flashed him a quick smile that hinted of nervousness as she twisted her hands together. Puzzled, he nodded toward the doorknob, but she surprised him by reaching out and ringing the doorbell.

THREE

Bill was right, Tammie thought. She needed serious therapy. In a week's time, she'd quit her job, traveled clear across the country and hooked up with a crazy man who'd led her to an old stone house in the middle of nowhere.

And she'd willingly followed him.

Heart pounding in her chest, she waited for someone to answer the bell. The bushes on both sides of the porch were tall, creating a tomblike enclosure in front of the door. A spring breeze shook the large shrubs and made a wind tunnel out of the covered entryway, adding to the cold dread consuming her. Old, dry leaves swirled around her feet.

Tammie turned and forced a smile at Dylan, darting a glance to the street, where her rental car sat parked. She could leave now, end this nonsense and beg to get her job back.

Sighing, she turned back to the door. Leaving now wouldn't change anything. There'd always be questions that needed answering. And until she got those answers, she wouldn't stop looking for them. She'd come this far. She had to go the distance.

Her hand was poised to ring the bell again, but the heavy, carved wooden door swung open.

Tammie didn't know what she'd expected to see on the other side of the door, but the shocked look on the face of the young woman who looked outside echoed what Tammie had felt in the pit of her stomach earlier, when she saw that picture of Serena Davco.

"Miss Serena? What are you doing outside?" the woman, wearing a maid's uniform, said. Her blond hair was pulled back and tucked underneath a white kerchief. The smell of lemon filtered out into the spring air. They'd probably interrupted her cleaning, Tammie surmised.

Confusion mixed with anxiety within Tammie as the young woman continued to stare with wide eyes, and Tammie lost her tongue for a moment.

"Is Serena Davco available?" Dylan said from behind her.

The woman looked past Tammie to where Dylan was standing and scowled. "You again? What have you done? Aurore will not be happy about this."

Something prickled the back of Tammie's neck. *Aurore.* Where had she heard that name before? "May we come in?"

The woman was obviously flabbergasted, but she stepped aside. "Of course."

Once inside, Tammie looked around. The wide foyer was richly decorated, with an old drop-leaf table that held a large colorful pottery vase with flowers. Tammie knew nothing about antiques, but the pieces she saw looked quite old, though they seemed to have been well cared for over the years. None of them matched the contemporary style Tammie normally favored, but the room just off the foyer held a homey elegance that was inviting.

Noise from the back of the house roused the young maid's attention.

"Susan?" a voice called out.

"Don't go anywhere," the woman said to Dylan, then disappeared down the hall to answer the call.

Within seconds, voices were raised, but Tammie found it hard to hear anything that was being said in the other room. She gave her attention to the room where she and Dylan had been left, taking in all the ornate details.

"Anything look familiar?" Dylan asked.

The mantel in the dining room, adjacent to the room they'd entered, caught Tammie's attention. There were pictures lined up along it. But as much as Tammie wanted to see the pictures, see the woman who lived in this house, they hadn't been invited to go any farther than the room they were in.

She turned to Dylan, who was leaning against the doorway with his arms folded. "No. Should it?"

"You live here."

He was probing her with his dark eyes.

Tammie's shoulders sagged. "I told you—"

"Yeah, your name is Tammie Gardner. I get that. But you're also Serena Davco. The question I'm asking myself is why you're continuing to use a different name? Why the pretense now that we're in familiar surroundings?"

She lifted her arms, but then let them fall to her sides again. "I don't know Serena Davco, and I've never been here before in my life. I'm just as curious about all this as you are."

"Yeah? If you're not Serena Davco, who do you suppose posed for that picture?"

Dylan pointed up the carpeted stairway, which led to a landing. Between two large stained-glass windows sat an enormous painting of a pregnant woman with a little girl with dark brown curls sitting on the floor beside her legs. The woman's face clearly matched her own. Even closer than the picture Dylan had showed her.

A chill raced up Tammie's spine, causing her to shiver.

"I have no idea. But you can be sure I'm going to find out."

The voices in the hallway grew louder.

"You just left her alone with him?"

An older woman charged into the foyer on the heels of the young maid, who Tammie guessed was Susan. A sense of déjà vu made her skin crawl. Nothing about this house or this town was familiar to Tammie—except this older woman. She'd seen her face somewhere before. Or rather, she'd seen the devastating scar that marred her cheek and neck. It had been sometime in her youth, but for the life of her, Tammie couldn't remember the details. All she remembered was how frightened she'd been.

The woman with the scar stopped short, eyes wide and gasped. "What on earth is going on here?"

"What—? We're here to see Serena Davco," Tammie said.

Although the woman tried to hide it, Tammie caught the almost imperceptible change in her expression before she shifted her attention to Dylan.

"You again?"

Tammie whispered to him, "Did anyone ever tell you that you have a funny way with people?"

"I get that a lot," Dylan said dryly, in a voice loud enough for all to hear.

"So you've had a run-in at this house before?" Tammie asked.

The scarred woman folded her arms across her chest. "I told you never to come here again."

"Yeah, you did. But this time I was invited."

"By whom?"

Dylan gestured toward Tammie.

"It's amazing, isn't it, Aurore?" Susan said in a hushed tone.

Eyeing Tammie again, the woman sneered. "You think bringing an imposter here is going to get you what you want? You're mistaken."

Tammie blinked at her hostility. "Imposter? No, no, my name is Tammie Gardner. I wasn't trying to fool anyone." Turning to Dylan, she said quietly, "What's going on here?"

"I don't care what your name is or what your intentions are. You both need to leave here immediately. Susan, call the police."

Dylan sputtered and took a step into the room. "What little law enforcement Eastmeadow has is tied up in the center of town, getting ready for the auctions. I came here to get some answers about my brother. As soon as I get them, I'll be sure to leave and not come back. Until then, we're not going anywhere."

"Aurore, Serena will be up soon," Susan said, darting a glance at the grand stairway.

"Go upstairs and check on her while I handle this."

"Aurore." Tammie reached out and touched the scarred woman's arm—a gesture she never would have made as a child, because disfigurement frightened her so. But the years suddenly melted away, and the memory of this woman standing in the kitchen with her mother came rushing back. An eerie sense of excitement filled her. "Of course. I remember that name. I remember you. You knew my parents…."

Susan stopped on the stairs and turned toward them, putting her hand to her mouth.

"Susan! Upstairs!" Aurore said urgently. Turning back to Tammie, she said, "You need to leave and never come back." The older woman gripped Tammie by the upper arm and firmly moved her toward the door, but Tammie held her ground.

"Connie and Aaron Gardner. You knew them. You came to the house one night. My mother was crying and you were trying to comfort her, but she never told me why. I heard her call you Aurore, and I asked her what that was. She told me about the northern lights. She wouldn't tell me why she was crying." Tammie's heart was pounding, and her eyes were fixed on Aurore's face. *"I remember you."*

"You're surely mistaken. I've never been to Oregon."

"I don't believe the lady ever mentioned she was from Oregon," Dylan said firmly, standing like a brick wall in front of the path to the door. "The only way I figure you'd know something like that is if what she's saying is true."

The grip on her arm eased a fraction as Aurore took a controlled breath.

"We moved to another house right after that. But you were definitely there, in Winchester."

It made sense now. After her parents' death, she'd gone back to the house in Winchester to try to figure out why they'd been acting so strangely at the end. But it was only now that she recalled the night Aurore had come to visit them.

"Did you go to see them again before they were killed? Is that why they wanted to leave on that boat trip so quickly?"

Aurore's face held no emotion, but when she spoke, her

voice was hard. "Neither one of you belong here. This is the Davco home. You're not welcome."

Tammie swallowed, found courage from somewhere deep in her soul. She glanced up at the painting on the wall, and then at the woman who so clearly wanted nothing to do with her. "Am I a Davco, as well? Tell me!"

"You certainly are."

The room seemed to lose its air as all eyes turned to the woman standing at the top of the stairway. From behind her, Dylan gasped. Seeing a picture, even the portrait on the wall was one thing. Seeing the woman face-to-face was totally amazing.

Susan stood behind the fragile woman at the top of the stairs, practically in tears. "Aurore, I tried to stop her…."

"I thought… This is unbelievable," Dylan said, expelling a quick breath.

Tammie stared at the woman, whose face was so much like her own and yet so different. The differences might be minor, but to Tammie they were distinctive. Serena Davco's nose had a slight hook at the tip, where hers was straight. The fullness of Tammie's face lacked the exotic air that Serena's thinner face seemed to have. They shared the same dark hair, cut at about the same length, but in different styles. Although they were tired-looking, Serena's eyes were a mirror image of her own. *The same eyes as the woman who sat with the little girl in the portrait.*

Tammie swallowed, nerves raising goose bumps on her arms.

"*You're* Serena Davco?" Dylan asked.

The woman pulled her terrycloth bathrobe tighter. "That's right."

Guilt stabbed at Tammie as she took in Serena's disheveled clothes and worn appearance. Still trembling, she said, "I'm sorry we disturbed you."

"Nonsense. I always enjoy company," she said, her voice slightly slurred. Then she chuckled softly. "And surprises."

"This is one huge surprise," Dylan chimed in from behind. "For me, anyway."

"They were just leaving, Miss Serena," Susan said, taking the woman by the upper arm. But Serena quickly wrenched away and gripped the banister.

"We have a few minutes to talk to the lady," Dylan said. "If you're up to it, that is."

Through tired eyes, Serena looked sharply at Susan, then at Aurore. Then she turned to Dylan and Tammie again. "They're always t-trying to keep me from company."

Aurore sighed impatiently. "You're not well, Serena. You need your rest. Now go with Susan to your room."

"It's my house. My company."

Serena swayed, and Susan grabbed her by the shoulders.

"You're both always hovering," she said, pulling away. "I'm f-fine."

She didn't look fine. Tammie was far from fine herself. The room seemed airless now, and Tammie fought to take each breath as she looked up into that face that looked so much like her own. "Maybe we should come back another time, when you're feeling better, Serena."

With disappointment in her eyes, Serena shook her head. "Oh, you can't leave now. I've been waiting for you."

"Susan, bring her to her room. It's the medication talking," Aurore said, turning to Tammie quickly.

The hair that framed the older woman's face drew

back, revealing the extent of her scarring. The fear Tammie had felt as a child, when she caught her first glimpse of that scar, came crashing back to her now, shaming her. Whatever had happened to Aurore to cause such a scar must have been devastating.

"She needs her rest," the woman said sharply.

"Don't leave. Please…s-say you won't leave," Serena pleaded from the top of the stairs.

Something stirred deep inside Tammie. She felt a connection with this woman so powerful that she threw out all reason. Her pulse thrummed at her temple. "I won't leave you, Serena."

Even as the words flew out of her mouth, uncertainty crashed forward, but she pushed it away. The answers she was looking for were here—as well as a whole slew of new questions.

Then Tammie remembered what the clerk at the hotel had said. "But there are no hotels—"

Serena's face grew brighter. "Oh, but there is plenty of room here! This house is as much yours as it is mine."

"Serena!" the scarred woman said. "You can't invite just anyone into the house."

Her determination seemed to make Serena stronger. "She's not just anyone. She's my s-sister. She belongs here!"

"No, Serena," Aurore said sympathetically. "The baby died in the fire that killed your mother. You've always known that."

Serena shook her head. "I heard the baby cry."

As Aurore continued to argue gently with Serena, Tammie stared at the portrait. A whirl of emotions coursed through her, and for a split second she had the urge to run from the house. How could this be happening?

From the outside, the mansion really did look as big as a hotel. But the only person welcoming her through the door was Serena, and it was clear that whatever medication she was taking was speaking for her.

Could this really be her sister? Yes, there was definitely a biological connection of some sort between her and Serena. A mere glance was all it took to confirm that. But her sister? If that was true, then who was the woman in the portrait with her?

Tammie swayed where she stood, finding it hard to breathe.

Ignoring the woman, Serena pushed forward and focused her attention on Tammie. "Please stay."

Tammie could feel Dylan standing behind her. Her heart pounded with fear that Serena would take one step too many and come toppling down the staircase. Everything about this house felt wrong, and yet she knew she had the truth staring her in the face. All she had to do was sort it out.

Lord, I don't know why this happened or what's going on. But I know You will lead me on the right path to find the truth. All I ask is that you keep me strong.

"Of course I'll stay," she said, pasting on a smile despite the uneasy feeling that flooded her. Her acceptance brightened Serena's gray face more than a fraction, and Tammie was glad for that.

"What are you doing, Tammie?" Dylan whispered from behind.

She turned to him, saw the worried lines deepening around his eyes. "I'm getting answers."

Aurore quickly strode up the stairs toward Serena, and Susan came rushing down. "If Serena insists on having her here, then get her bags—quickly, while I bring Serena back to bed." She nodded sharply at Dylan. "Make sure *he* leaves."

As Serena and Aurore disappeared upstairs, Susan led them to the front door. "I'll wait here while you get your bags. Any visiting will have to wait until Serena is feeling better."

"What's wrong with her?" Dylan asked as he walked out the door.

"She's not well."

He stopped, turned and Tammie almost collided with the wall of his back. "Obviously."

Susan lifted her chin in defiance. "Aurore has asked me to—"

"Yeah, I heard. I'm to leave," Dylan said. He glanced at Tammie.

Susan continued. "Just because you've made your way through the front door, that doesn't mean you're privy to family business."

"Am I family? Really?" Tammie asked.

"Serena seems to think so," Dylan said.

Susan cast them a long look, then said, with a sigh that seemed to weigh her down, "She's suffered from mental illness her whole life. It's only gotten worse since Byron Davco, her father, was diagnosed with Alzheimer's. He's been in a nursing home for over a year now. The loss has been too much for her to handle."

Tammie wanted to cry—for Serena and her loss, and because she knew that kind of loss, as well. She had longed for a sister her whole life and now it seemed she'd always had one. Right now, though, exhaustion was winning out over curiosity.

Part of her had held on to the notion that maybe her parents hadn't known she wasn't their biological daughter, as Bill had suggested. But now that she'd met Aurore and remembered her visit as a child, Tammie doubted that. They'd known.

Lord, I know You won't give me a bigger burden than I can handle. Please help me find out why my parents kept this from me. Please give me the strength to see this through.

"Why don't you get your bags, so I can show you to your room?" Susan said impatiently.

They'd walked a few yards down the pathway toward the street when Dylan caught her arm.

"Tammie?"

His face was dark, and his troubled eyes bored into her with what she might have called fear in anyone else. But the man she'd met earlier hadn't been afraid of her running him over with her car. She doubted he feared anything.

Pressing her fingers against her throbbing temple, she said, "I finally understand what you meant by feeling like you're in some weird science fiction movie."

"Your staying at this house will only make it worse. This isn't a good idea," he said quietly. "I should never have brought you here."

She had to look up at him. In such close proximity, she saw how much taller he was than her, smelled the clean scent of him minus the strong odor of shaving cologne that most men seemed to bathe in.

She sighed, then turned to Susan, who was waiting for her. "Give me a minute to get my suitcase, and then you can show me to my room."

When they were off the porch, she voiced her thoughts. "You're wrong, Dylan. I didn't know exactly what I was searching for or what I'd find when I drove into town this morning. Now I know. All the answers I'm looking for start here—in this house."

Dylan's eyes darted back to the mansion and then to Tammie again. "It doesn't feel right. Cash said he was coming here to save Serena. I thought he was being dramatic, but that's out of character for my brother. Now I feel like I've just thrown you to the wolves. I can't leave you here like this."

She cocked her head to one side and paused as they reached her car. "You were so eager to get me here in the first place. Why the change?"

He looked away, seeming embarrassed, but then looked her square in the eye. She admired him for that.

"I'm sorry. I thought you were playing games with me. It's my suspicious nature. In my line of work, I'm used to people feeding me lines. I spent all these weeks here getting the runaround, and then you showed up. When I saw you out on that road, I didn't believe you. Even as we drove here I thought you were really Serena Davco."

She nodded and smiled as she yanked open the door to the backseat of her rental car. "I'm not in the habit of lying, Dylan. *That's* not *my* nature."

Dylan grabbed her suitcase and then slammed the door. "I'm not, either. And I didn't trust your word, and I'm sorry for that, too. Look, I don't know what brought you here, but I have a feeling we're both after the same thing—the truth. I'm just not comfortable with you staying here alone."

A warm flow of emotion hugged her. "It's sweet of you

to worry. But I'm not going to be alone here. I've just found out I have a sister. No DNA tests are going to tell me different."

"It's not safe."

"How do you know that?"

He looked at her hard. "Because my brother is missing. I don't want you to be, too."

Tammie glanced back to the house and caught the sharp glance Susan cast at them from the front door as she waited for Tammie to return. It was clear they didn't want Dylan there. No one but Serena wanted Tammie there, but it was a harder argument for the others to win when it was clear Serena Davco believed Tammie was her long-lost sister, who had supposedly died at birth.

With a quick rake of his hand over his head, Dylan looked back at the house and grunted. "We can come back tomorrow. Maybe Serena will be feeling better then. Call it gut instinct, but I don't like what's happening here."

Tammie couldn't have agreed more. But she shook her head, determined to see this through. "That's not good enough."

"Sometimes that's all you have. Cash is missing because he went after Serena Davco, and it's clear they've made a fortress out of this place to keep people from her."

"Exactly the reason I should stay."

"You have a name now, information to start searching for the truth. You don't have to be here to do it."

"What about you? Serena knew your brother."

Dylan reached for her, touching her shoulder. The warmth of his touch, the gentle concern in his eyes, filled her with emotion. "And my brother disappeared."

Voices from an upstairs window filtered out into the summer air, but Tammie couldn't make out the words. "Aurore knew my mother and father. Ever since I found out they weren't my biological parents, I've been having a hard time forgiving them for not telling me the truth. I've been praying but I can't get past it."

A look passed between them, a look she didn't quite understand, and held for a moment.

"Ms. Gardner," Susan called from the front porch. "If you're ready, I'll show you to your room."

Dylan sighed and pulled the envelope with Serena's picture and a pen out of his shirt pocket. He tore off a piece of the envelope and wrote something on it.

"This place gets weirder and weirder. Take this. It's my cell number and the name of the campground I'm staying at in town. It's not the lap of luxury, but there's room there, and it's clean. You might want to consider changing your mind."

She took the slip of paper from him and was surprised by how much her hand was shaking. She fought to steady it.

"You came all the way from Chicago to go camping?"

"It's going to take more than getting thrown out of my hotel room because of the auction to get me to leave town. I *will* get the information I need to find Cash." He hesitated. "And I *won't* leave until I know you're going to be okay alone."

She shifted in place, looked away and then straight at him. Fear of what was to come suddenly came crashing in around her.

"Are you okay?" he asked, reaching out and taking her by the arm.

"You could stay, too," she said, tears filling her eyes. She wouldn't cry. It wouldn't help anything if she did. She was just tired.

"No one gave me an invitation. And since Aurore and her shadow have spent the last month making sure I don't darken their doorstep, it's not likely I'll get one."

The idea of being here alone, without an ally, didn't sit well with her, but what choice did she really have? Every hotel was booked solid.

Dylan was a handsome man, when he wasn't looking at her all crazy and determined. And, even in that state Tammie had to admit, there was something strangely appealing about him. He had a strength that made her feel safe, a determination and sense of honor where his brother was concerned, that she could only admire.

"Dylan, you didn't get me into this. You probably wouldn't have been the only one assuming I was Serena Davco. I most likely would have made my way right here on my own. I'm not your responsibility."

"Right."

He didn't sound convinced. Maybe it was the cop in him who felt the need to protect her.

"Why haven't you gone to the local police regarding your suspicions about Cash?"

He sputtered and shook his head. "What there is in terms of law enforcement in this town is a joke. Besides, no one besides me believes anything sinister has happened to Cash."

"Look. It took you a month to get this far. I'm not going to leave now and risk having them slam the door in my face the next time I come to talk to Serena."

Dylan sighed, defeated. "If you're stubborn enough to

want to stay, I can't stop you. Call me if you need anything. I don't care what time it is. I *will* be back tomorrow morning."

To her surprise, those few words gave her comfort.

"At least you know I'll answer the door and let you in."

He smiled and gave her a wave as he walked away. She watched him climb into his Jeep and drive away before dragging her bag toward the door.

"This way," Susan said.

Tammie followed her up the stairs and paused on the landing to stare at the picture of the pregnant woman with the young child.

"What was her name?"

Susan stopped and glanced back at Tammie. "Eleanor."

Tears filled Tammie's eyes. "And the baby?"

"The baby died inside the womb with her mother during the fire."

No she didn't, Tammie thought. *Not if what Serena believes is true.* She clamped her teeth over her bottom lip.

"Is that how Aurore was scarred? In the fire?"

Susan glared. "Maybe you should be asking Aurore that."

You can count on that, Tammie thought.

FOUR

Loud cries from the other side of the bedroom wall jolted Tammie from her sleep. Serena was screaming!

Tossing her light cotton robe over her shoulders, she tied the sash and hurried to the bedroom door. Aurore and Susan were already running toward Serena's room when she stepped into the hall.

"Go back to bed," Aurore said, dismissing her.

Tammie ignored her request and followed them. "What's wrong with her?"

"Just a nightmare," Susan said, blocking the doorway after Aurore entered. "She frequently has them. Go back to bed. We'll take care of it."

The sounds of glass being broken and items dropping to the floor echoed loudly through the quiet night. Loud crashes and the scraping of wood against wood had Tammie looking over Susan's shoulder into the room. Serena was now crouched in the corner, her hands pressed against her face and she was sobbing uncontrollably. A tall dresser was turned on its side, the drawers pulled out and clothes spilled on the floor.

Unable to stay back, she pushed past Susan and stepped

into the room. Clothes were everywhere. Pictures were strewn all over the bed and on the floor. Tammie reached down and picked up a photograph. She immediately recognized the man holding Serena in a warm embrace as Cash Montgomery.

"This looks like it's more than a simple nightmare. She's clearly very upset."

Aurore crouched down next to Serena, giving Tammie a pointed stare. "This is not your concern. We'll handle this."

"Serena?" Tammie moved toward the young woman, who had yet to acknowledge that any of them were even in the room. Susan's hand held her back.

"I agreed to your staying here in this house only because Serena insisted on it."

"You didn't agree to anything. Serena wanted me here."

"I've helped to run this house since Serena was a little girl. When Mr. Davco went into the nursing home, he left *me* in charge. If I felt strong enough that you shouldn't be here, you wouldn't be. Clearly this has upset Serena. Perhaps it's best that you leave first thing in the morning and go back to wherever you came from before—"

"Before what? Before I talk to Serena? Before she tells me something you don't want me to know?"

Susan's hand tightened on her arm. "You have no right—"

"Susan!" Aurore interjected.

Tammie wrenched free of Susan's hold and advanced into the room. Aurore stood up straight, but did not offer any resistance.

Not normally one to be so bold, Tammie was surprised that she'd found the courage to stand up to them.

Perhaps it was because they seemed so strangely protective of Serena.

It was unquestionably true that Serena was in a delicate state. The last thing Tammie wanted to do was make her condition worse. But she couldn't help but think that her visit had been the cause of this outburst tonight. Nightmare? If that was truly what it was, it was worse than any nightmare Tammie had ever heard of. And she wanted to know, what had caused Serena to become so upset?

"Serena?" Tammie said, reaching to take her hand. She pulled her own hand back immediately, gasping softly, when she realized it was wet. Blood was smeared on her palm and fingers. "You're bleeding!"

"What?" Aurore turned Serena's wrists over. The angry gash, wet with blood, clearly startled her.

"Susan, get the first aid kit immediately," Aurore commanded, pulling Serena to her feet.

Tammie pressed her palm against the wound to help stop the bleeding.

"She didn't hit a vein, or it'd be worse," Aurore said with controlled calm.

Still, blood was seeping from between Tammie's fingers. Upon closer inspection, Tammie saw drops of blood staining the turned-over dresser, as well.

"I…broke…the bottle," Serena said, shaking her head.

"Be careful of the glass," Tammie said to her. "You're barefoot."

Her face registered no response and no pain. But looking at the glass on the floor and the fragments of the broken bottle, Tammie knew the gash had to sting, especially because the contents of the bottle—perfume—surely would have seeped into the wound when the bottle broke.

"Why did she do this?" Tammie asked when they finally got Serena safely into bed.

"She didn't do it on purpose," Aurore said, examining Serena's wrist. Then she sighed, as if she were relieved. "It's just a surface wound. It could have been worse. Serena, why did you get out of bed? You could have really hurt yourself this time."

"How often does this happen?" Tammie asked her.

"She has nightmares. She doesn't know what she's doing. She probably won't even remember this in the morning."

Serena's quiet sobs and vacant stare as she looked around the room stopped Tammie's heart. This was what people meant when they said "the lights are on but no one is home," she thought. She'd never seen it before. Not like this, anyway.

Both Aurore and Tammie were checking Serena's feet to see if there were any cuts from the glass, checking her nightgown to make sure there was nothing stuck to it. And Serena was complying without any fight. Tammie wasn't sure Serena even knew there was anyone in the room with her, let alone two people putting her back in the four-poster bed and covering her with a heavy blanket.

Aurore turned to Tammie, visibly shaken. Her trembling hand brushed a fallen strand of hair away from her face, revealing her deep scar. "If you're going to be here, I could use some help righting the dresser and cleaning up the glass. But you'll want to get some slippers, so that you're not walking on the floor in your bare feet. We don't need two people getting cut tonight."

"I'll be careful," Tammie replied. She reached down and picked up a picture frame that had fallen off the dresser. The glass was broken but the elderly man in the picture with Serena caught Tammy's attention. "Who's this?"

Aurore looked at the picture quickly. "Byron Davco, Serena's father. It was taken before he went into the nursing home."

Tammie looked at the picture again. "I'd like to go visit him."

"What on earth for?" Aurore asked.

"He may be able to tell me something about my parents."

"His Alzheimer's is too advanced. He doesn't even remember Serena. I doubt he could give you any information that would be useful to you. Now, please help me with this."

The two of them righted the dresser just as Susan came into the room with the first aid kit.

Serena lay still in the bed, whimpering. And she gave no response to the heavy bang of the dresser's feet hitting the pine floor. She just continued to whimper, even as Aurore came back to her side by the bed.

Tammie held Serena's wounded hand up to keep the blood from dripping on the bed. Serena quickly turned and grabbed Tammie's other hand. "They're stealing babies. They steal little babies," she said, and then began sobbing, falling back onto her pillow. Tammie took her hand and squeezed it.

Susan dropped the first aid kit on the other side of the bed and opened it.

"I can take care of her from here," Aurore said. The tone of her voice had changed from the way it had been earlier.

"What does she mean about stealing babies?" Tammie pressed. "Is she talking about me?"

"Go back to Oregon, Tammie," Aurore said, heaving a heavy sigh and shaking her head. "Please. No good can come from you being here."

Although she was uneasy about leaving Serena, she nodded.

As she walked through Serena's bedroom door, she heard Aurore say, "Make sure you lock your door."

She turned around, but Aurore had her full attention on Serena.

Tammie walked back to her room, hearing Serena's quiet sobs at her back as she moved. Every once in a while, a floorboard would creak beneath her bare foot, seeming to echo in the hallway.

She stopped at her door and turned back again. The upstairs was illuminated now that everyone in the house was awake. The cold light above her was as harsh and unwelcome as she felt.

Had her visit done this to Serena? Tammie couldn't help but think that somehow it had. While Aurore hadn't been as cold to her tonight as she had been earlier, there was a definite chill in the air when Tammie was around. Aurore had made it clear she still didn't want her in this house, despite Serena's wishes. And Serena wasn't really in any shape to voice her true wishes anymore.

Walking through the doorway, Tammie closed the bedroom door and locked it, as requested. But that didn't make her feel any more secure.

She saw long streaks of light stretching into the room. The heavy brocade drapes were opened wide, letting in the light of the bright moon.

She usually liked her room in pitch darkness. But not

tonight. She needed light. *Or enlightenment.* But she knew that wouldn't come just because she wanted it.

The fact that she'd been woken from a dead sleep earlier surprised Tammie. She was still on West Coast time, and she normally went to bed late, doing paperwork at the kitchen table, for lack of a social life to keep her busy. A quick glance at the clock told her it was two-thirty in the morning—eleven-thirty West Coast time. If she was home, she probably wouldn't even be ready for bed.

Pulling off her robe, she plopped down on the edge of the bed, intending to crawl back in and see if sleep would claim her, as it had earlier. She should be dead on her feet, but there were too many questions rolling around her head. She'd thought she had questions before she left Oregon. Now they'd multiplied tenfold.

She wouldn't give them any more thought, or at least she'd try not to. If she didn't get back to sleep now, she'd end up being in bed until noon. She wanted to be fresh in the morning, so she could talk with Serena. And after tonight, she hoped Serena would be in a good enough state to talk.

Replacing one thought only led to another that seemed equally disturbing. *Dylan*, she thought with a stir of awareness. He was…interesting. He wasn't the type of man she'd normally be drawn to. He was a bit too gruff for her liking. She didn't like men who were pushy and arrogant. And what kind of man stands in the middle of the road waiting for someone to run him down?

Nuts! The guy was truly nuts.

And yet, she couldn't stop thinking of him. He'd shown a different side, as well. His concern for his brother Cash was endearing. It was clear that they were close and that he loved his family.

His sudden concern for her when she'd made the decision to stay at the mansion puzzled Tammie. Why would he care? They'd only just met. And yet his concern appeared to be so genuine. There was more to this man than the rough exterior he displayed.

She sighed, closed her eyes and offered a short prayer to the Lord that her mother had taught her when she was a little girl. *For this new morning with its light, for rest and shelter of the night, for health and food, for love of friends, for everything Thy goodness sends...Lord in heaven, we thank Thee.*

Then she laughed quietly and shook her head. "For crying out loud, he's just a guy," she said to herself. "It's not like he's Keanu Reeves or—"

Tammie stopped short. Why was she thinking about Dylan Montgomery at all? There was something about him that had stuck with her.

"Yeah, it's that the guy is nuts," she decided. She already had enough in her life to deal with, and she didn't need to add a guy who was clearly on the wrong side of normal.

The only reason he was of interest to her was that his brother and Serena were somehow connected. Maybe they *could* help each other.

Instead of crawling back into bed, Tammie padded to the window. Resting her palms on the windowsill, she stared out into the backyard. She couldn't see much because the moon had dipped beyond the shadow of the tall pine trees that lined the yard. Reaching wide, she clutched the heavy drapes and began to close them, only to stop when she heard an odd sound and caught the image of a dark form crouched down near the stone wall.

Eastmeadow was out in the middle of nowhere, and there were sure to be a lot of wild animals around. The figure was too large to be a dog. A bear? Were there bears in Western Massachusetts? Tammie supposed so. She'd seen some in the hills of Oregon while she'd been on vacation once. Why not Massachusetts?

She thought of Dylan staying at the campground. The thought of sleeping while wild animals lurked outside the tent gave her the creeps. Even being in a camper wouldn't give her the same sense of security as being on the second floor of a house.

The figure moved and then stood up. Since it was in the shadows, she couldn't make out the details until it moved into the light of the moon and turned its face toward the house, looking up at her window.

With a gasp, Tammmie stepped back into the shadows of the curtain.

That was no bear outside in the garden.

It was a man. A man holding a shovel.

He'd lucked out in one way, Dylan thought as he looked at his clean face in the little mirror. At least he had running water.

He dropped his razor into the sink and swished it back and forth to clean it.

Okay, it wasn't hot. He'd had to warm it in a pan on the propane stove. But he didn't have to haul water in like some of the campers who'd checked into the campground after him, either.

By sheer good timing, he'd managed to snag the last camper from Julius, and he'd be eternally grateful for that. While the walls of the camper weren't thick, they did afford a little bit of soundproofing. That was a good thing, because his neighbors in the next campsite had decided that quiet hours didn't apply to them.

After inspecting his chin to make sure he hadn't missed any spots, he set the mirror down on the small counter. He splashed his face with the lukewarm water to wash away the residual soap, blotting it dry with the SpongeBob SquarePants terry towel he had bought from the camp's store and now had wrapped around his shoulders.

He didn't need a second look in the mirror at his tired eyes. The camper's bed was comfortable enough. He'd slept on a lot of cots and on the ground in his years with the Marines. He'd learned to do without comfort in exchange for rest. He could sleep on a rock, if he needed to, and still be refreshed. It hadn't been the bed that kept him tossing all night.

Tammie Gardner. Now she was a surprise he hadn't counted on. Who'd have thought Serena had a sister?

He certainly hadn't.

He wasn't sure he liked this surprise. He was used to being in control. He had to be. Whether in a foreign land with his unit or on the streets of Chicago, he needed to stay in control.

He hadn't been yesterday. *Not by a long shot.* That wasn't a habit he wanted to continue. He wasn't normally one to get broadsided, and he had been yesterday—in a big way—when he met Tammie.

There had been more than a few women in his life over the years. Some had been more of a challenge than others.

But living overseas and constantly going wheels up on a black op made it difficult to have any kind of lasting relationship. The idea of waiting her life away, not knowing where her man is or if he's even coming home, hadn't been too appealing to most of the women he'd dated.

He couldn't say he blamed them. Still, he was thirty-seven years old and still without a family of his own.

Most of the time, that didn't bother Dylan. He'd had a full life in the military. Whenever he thought of his life, he had no regrets. It was fulfilling, serving God and his country.

But lately, mostly since he'd come home and seen how preoccupied Cash had been, he'd begun to wonder if he'd traded in the good part of life. He hadn't been ready for a family, couldn't imagine fitting a wife and kids into his crazy schedule. But raising a family in a loving, Christian home, as his parents had done, had always been in the back of his mind. One of those "someday" things—but "someday" had kind of snuck up on him.

He tried to shrug it off as he pulled the plug and watched the soapy water drain. Some of the women he'd dated in college had been married for years now. A few even had kids who were starting high school.

He blew out a quick breath. "High school," he muttered, and grabbed a paper towel to wipe the water that had gotten all over the counter.

Where had the time gone? It didn't seem like fourteen years since he'd graduated college. Twelve years in the military seemed like a blink of an eye now. He could remember every soldier he'd ever worked with on a mission. He'd needed to. They'd had to depend on each other, whether they liked each other or not.

As for the women in his life, well, *that* was a bit blurry. Although it had never bothered Dylan before, it wasn't sitting so well with him now. He was suddenly wondering just when he'd become the kind of guy to take a woman's affection for granted.

He could blame his fitful night of sleep on a lot of things. Worry over what had happened to Cash was on the top of the list. Being in different surroundings would have been a good excuse, but it made no sense, given his life in the military.

And then there was Tammie Gardner. He still couldn't believe she'd actually stayed at the mansion last night. She was crazy! It didn't matter that she was practically a mirror image of Serena. She didn't know those people. Anything could have happened.

It wasn't Dylan's place to tell Tammie what she should and shouldn't do, and he had a good-enough picture of the woman to know she probably wouldn't appreciate him doing it. But it hadn't kept him from worrying about her last night, even though he'd only met her less than twenty-four hours ago.

And yet, even after such a short period of time, he couldn't get Tammie out of his mind.

He shook his head as if to shake her memory from his mind and sat on the bed, pulling his boots in front of him to put them on. He slipped both his feet inside and began lacing the first boot.

"Twilight zone," he muttered as he worked. "I could plead insanity, too. This town is a good enough excuse for that."

He finished getting dressed, pulling on a favorite T-shirt that his mom always threatened to throw out because it was so old.

He was debating about whether to eat some breakfast

before heading over to the Davco mansion or wait and invite Tammie out to join him when he heard a car pull into the spot next to his Jeep.

Curious, Dylan pushed aside the faded curtains on the small window to see if it was Julius. To his surprise, he was met with a smile and a wave. The person sitting in the front seat of the car had a nicer smile than the campground owner; he wasn't quite sure he liked the effect that smile had on his gut.

Pushing the camper door open, he stepped outside just as Tammie got out of the car and shut the door. She looked around, and then her gaze fell on him.

"What happened?" he asked, stepping out onto the gravel driveway of the campsite.

She looked at him, seeming puzzled. "Nothing. What makes you think something has happened?"

He glanced at the sky. "I don't have my watch on, but I can guess it's pretty early. There had to be something that drove you from the house to come and seek me out. Especially since just yesterday you tried to run me down with your car."

She gave a sheepish grin. "I did do that, didn't I?"

"Yes, you did."

Tammie nodded. "Well, stranger things have happened."

"Such as?"

Her brows furrowed. "Boy, you just get right down to things, don't you? Not even a mention of coffee—which, by the way, I haven't had and am dying for right now. In case you forgot, I'm still on Oregon time."

With a shrug, he said, "No coffee, I'm afraid. I didn't have a chance to pick up anything for the kitchen yesterday."

She gave a mock pout and snapped her fingers in disappointment.

He added, "We can get some at the campground store, or just run down to the café for breakfast. Take your pick."

Tammie lifted her eyes to him and held her gaze. "There was a man in the yard last night."

"A man? Outside the house?"

"Yes."

He laughed humorlessly. "And you say *I* cut to the chase. We went from coffee to a man in the backyard?"

She sighed and rubbed the back of her neck. "I haven't had coffee yet. My mind is a little fuzzy."

"What was he doing?"

"I don't really know. It looked like he was digging."

"In the dirt?"

With a roll of her eyes, she said, "Where else?"

"Did anyone else hear or see him? Any of the other people in the house?"

"They should have heard him. He was making enough noise for me to hear him from the second floor. But Serena had had a nightmare, and they were so busy with her, they probably didn't notice."

His brow creased. "Did the man try to come near the house?"

"Not the house. But he did go into a shed out back."

Dylan nodded. He'd never gone out back. He'd never even made it past the front door before yesterday. But with all the trees surrounding the property, and the desolate country roads that led up to the mansion, it would be easy for someone to get in and out of the yard unseen.

Tammie was leaning against her car, her arms folded across her chest and her head bent slightly.

He cleared his throat. "Did you say anything to anyone?"

Another roll of the eyes. "Do you think I would have gotten a straight answer if I had?"

"Point taken. But still, if someone is searching the grounds in the middle of the night, whoever it is might get bold enough to try to get into the house."

Looking alarmed, Tammie stood straight and unfolded her arms.

He answered the unspoken question written on her face. "That mansion is like a fortress, but people have been known to break into buildings with even the tightest security systems."

"I wonder if that had happened before," she said, her eyes shifting to one side, as if she were thinking of something.

He waited, and when her eyes met his again, she said, "Aurore told me to lock my bedroom door last night."

"Strange."

"I thought so, too. The only people I could think to worry about last night were Susan and Aurore. That is, until I saw the man in the garden."

Dylan looked more closely at Tammie then, saw the droop of her posture, the dark lines under her blue eyes, which were puffy, as if she hadn't had much sleep.

Well, at least he hadn't been the only one.

"There's time enough to ask them about it later," he said. "Why don't you take a load off while I pick up some things from the campground store? We can throw together some breakfast here. Carol, the waitress at the diner, is a sweet girl, but she has big ears. She can retell a conversation verbatim to the other waitresses the moment her customers walk out the door."

Tammie laughed. "I see your point. Besides, given the fact that Serena is practically my double, I'd rather the whole world not come to the conclusion that I'm her."

"If they haven't already," Dylan added.

FIVE

Tammie sat at the picnic table at the campsite while Dylan walked to the campground store. She was still on West Coast time, and the hour she'd gotten out of bed this morning was totally illegal, as far as her body's clock was concerned. But it hadn't made much sense to stay in a bed that wasn't even hers, when she couldn't sleep.

The house had been quiet when she left. Serena had still been in bed. If Aurore was around, she hadn't seen her. As Tammie came down the stairs, she'd seen Susan carrying a load of freshly laundered towels, but she didn't think Susan had seen her.

Not that it mattered. She wasn't hiding from anyone. But she had given a moment's thought to whether or not they'd let her back in the door when she returned. It wasn't as if she had a key.

Tammie was half in a daze, her fist propped under her chin and her elbow resting on the table, when she heard whistling. She turned to see Dylan walking up the dirt trail, carrying two paper bags brimming with groceries. Tammie lifted herself from the position she'd been sitting in and met him halfway down the trail to retrieve one of the bags.

"Thanks," he said with a smile.

"Are you always this chipper in the morning?"

He glanced at the sky. "No, not always. But I figure there's a blue sky and a bright sun hanging over me. The birds were singing as my eyes opened, and kids were playing in the park across from the store. That makes it a good day. If you've seen as many foreign lands as I have, witnessed the carnage that can go on in the world, you learn to take these things as a gift from God and praise Him for allowing you to bear witness to it."

Tammie smiled, almost ashamed that her mood had remained glum and she hadn't taken notice of the day like Dylan had.

"You're right." She bounced the bag in her arms. "What do you have in here, anyway—textbooks? It's so heavy!"

"I just about grabbed everything I could get my hands on. I'm a bit hungry," he said, shrugging. "I skipped dinner last night."

"Ah. My mother always said to never go shopping on an empty stomach." She stopped short at the memory. But Dylan didn't seem to notice how the mention of her mother affected her.

He opened the camper door and stepped inside, holding the door for her to follow. "Omelets okay with you?" he asked.

"Perfect. Need help cooking?"

"Why, are you a good cook?"

She chuckled. "Passable. But no one has ever complained."

"That's good enough for me."

The camper was an older model, with a bedroom in the

far end and a tight living room and kitchen area. At least it afforded enough elbow room that two people didn't have to bump into each other every time they turned around.

Tammie opened the cabinet above the stove and found an assortment of plastic dishes and cups in a variety of colors. She pulled out the four-cup coffeemaker and set it on the counter.

"I hope you bought a lot of coffee. We're going to need a refill on this."

Dylan chuckled and lit the pilot light on the burner. As he began whipping eggs and pouring them into a buttered pan, Tammie filled the coffeemaker and looked for the largest mugs she could find.

Questions that had been rolling around in her head the night before started to become clearer again as the smell of coffee filled her senses.

"What happened to your brother?" she finally asked.

Dylan stirred the eggs, seeming to weigh his words as he thought. It made Tammie wonder all the more about what a former Marine turned Chicago cop was doing in this small Massachusetts town. What could have happened to Cash to bring him out here?

"You don't know my brother," he finally said.

"So tell me about him."

He shook his head. "You won't understand what I'm trying to say." His voice was low, betraying a worry that Tammie was sure he felt every day. If someone she loved went missing, she didn't know how she'd handle it.

"What's the problem?"

He stopped stirring the eggs, turned off the burner and grabbed the plates Tammie had put down next to the stove.

"It's not that easy to explain the kind of man Cash is. Without that, I'll end up sounding like I'm defending him. He doesn't need defending. There are those who'd just as soon hang him as look at what I see in him."

Startled, she turned directly to him. "Hang him?"

He stopped short, pausing with the pan over a half-filled plate of eggs, then resumed. "That's just a figure of speech. But trust me, sometimes it feels like a lynching. You see, despite Cash never being in the military, he had a way about him that always reminded me of a code. Honor and respect are at his core."

"Both are traits to admire."

"Yes. Even though he's always been good at taking care of himself, I'm afraid he let his judgment of others slip."

She lowered her eyes and then raised them back to him. "You mean with Serena."

"Among others. If you don't know him like I know him, it's easy to come to the same conclusion as everyone else."

"I'm not like everyone else."

"I believe that about you." And then he looked at her directly and smiled.

Tammie fought hard to keep from showing her surprise. Bill always challenged her thinking. Told her she was being ridiculous where her suspicions were concerned. It was refreshing to hear someone say he believed her.

"Tell me about Cash."

"He's a good man, Tammie. I'm not saying he didn't get into his share of mischief when he was a kid. We both riled up our parents pretty often with our pranks, and my mom attributes all her grays to us." He flashed a quick grin.

"That's just kid stuff. I'll bet most mothers of boys will say the same thing."

"Exactly. But there are some people in the DEA that are trying to paint Cash in a bad way."

"He was in the Drug Enforcement Administration?"

Dylan nodded. "What they're saying just doesn't add up to the man I know."

She smiled. "It *does* sound like you're defending him. You don't have to do that."

Dropping the empty pan into the sink, he picked up the plates of scrambled eggs. "Well, there are a whole lot of people judging him. Or they would be, if they could find him."

"What do you mean?"

"Let me back up. Sonny—that's my kid sister, Sonia— had written to me when I was overseas that something funny was going on with Cash. She couldn't quite put a finger on what it was and for a long time I just thought she was exaggerating. I mean, she was a kid, just finished high school. I thought it was just drama."

She took a paper plate and stacked the buttered toast she'd prepared while Dylan talked. She put it on the table, and poured the black coffee. She motioned to indicate the milk in her hand.

"A little bit, thanks," he replied.

After stirring the coffees, she brought them to the table and sat down opposite him.

"He never said anything to you about what was going on?"

"Not a word. Not to Sonny, my parents or me. It's hard to read between the lines in letters. So Sonny made it plain one day, sending me a letter that just said I needed to come home. Now.

"The timing was right. I was getting ready to reenlist for another four years. Had the paperwork all filled out, just not submitted to my CO. I decided to come stateside instead. It wasn't until I got here that I saw how right Sonny was."

Tammie was struck by how openly Dylan talked about his family. It was clear that he held them all in great regard and that they cared for each other. It was refreshing. Too often, she'd met men who preferred to strike out on their own. Family life became a token visit once a year, during the holidays.

She'd grown up as an only child. While Tammie had many friends she was close to, she'd missed the kind of relationship one could have with a sibling, and she wondered if that would have helped with the loneliness she felt after her parents' deaths.

"If he didn't say anything, how did you know?"

Dylan's face changed. She tried to read his expression, but he showed his pain for only a brief moment and then it was gone.

"He wouldn't look me in the eye."

When she didn't say anything, he shook his head and went on. "You have to understand, we're brothers. No matter what, Cash and I had never kept secrets from each other. We were partners in crime growing up."

He seemed to wince at his own words, as if he'd realized what he'd said, and he paused for a moment. His voice was low when he continued.

"From the time we were able to walk, we shared everything. We roomed together, from the cradle all the way through college, until I went into the Marines. You learn things about a person when you're lying in the dark like that. You're not afraid to say things when you think no one is looking at you, judging you." He pointed to her eggs. "You should eat before that gets cold."

Tammie had been so engrossed in the conversation that she hadn't even touched her breakfast. She picked up her fork, but just pushed the food around on the plate.

"Do you have any sisters or brothers?"

Tammie thought of Serena. "I didn't grow up with any siblings." Just saying the words pierced her heart. What family she knew was dead. Except…

She wouldn't go there. There was no evidence, other than what she'd seen at the Davco mansion. Looking like Serena and her mother didn't make them immediate family. For all she knew, Serena was a distant relative. She couldn't get her hopes up that Serena was her sister.

Dylan nodded. "Family is important. It has a way of keeping you steady. When you grow up with a brother or a sister, you just know things about them that aren't expressed in words. Something was up with Cash, something he didn't want anyone to know. And Serena Davco is at the core of it."

His face grew hard, but she knew his anger wasn't aimed at her. He clearly blamed Serena for his brother's disappearance.

"Why do you think I'd judge Cash?"

He looked at her directly now, a flash of anger striking his eyes and then disappearing. "Because he's being judged by everyone, and now hunted down like a dog because of it."

"I don't understand."

Dylan sighed, dropped his fork and sat back in his seat. "He was arrested a few months ago for drug trafficking."

"Oh, I see." She hadn't expected anything like that.

"No, you really don't. He didn't do what they said he did."

"Your loyalty to him is admirable. I'm sure I would—"

"He didn't do it," he insisted. "You see, it's not just that I love my brother and know he could never be a party to giving drugs to kids. It's more than that."

"That is what they've accused him of?"

"More or less."

Trying to remain neutral, Tammie tried to take the side of reason. "There must have been some evidence that led the authorities to that conclusion." When he just stared, she added. "I'm not saying I don't believe you. I'm just wondering how the authorities could have charged him with a crime as serious as drug trafficking if they didn't have some kind of evidence against him. I'm just trying to understand it from your point of view."

That would be impossible, and Tammie knew it. She didn't know Cash. She didn't love him the way Dylan did. And she didn't have the unconditional trust that came from living and sharing a home with someone all your life.

Dylan seemed to understand the tack she was taking. "My brother was DEA. Had been for years. He'd made a trip to Colombia not long ago. He said it was business, but…" He scratched his head. "The people at the DEA said he didn't have business in Colombia, and he didn't say anything to me. He traveled a lot. Mostly out to the East Coast. But that wasn't unusual. It was part of his job. The prosecutor is claiming that the only business he had in Colombia was to arrange to bring drugs into the country."

"The prosecutor just pulled that out of thin air?" she said delicately.

Dylan leaned back in the seat and scrubbed his hand over his head, leaving his hair slightly disheveled. "They found a stash in his apartment."

When she didn't say anything, he added, "Cash was framed."

"You know that for sure?"

"I'd been at his apartment the night before. Since I'd been back in the States, I watched his place when he traveled."

"Collect the mail and feed the fish?" she said.

He smiled for the first time since the conversation about his brother started. "Something like that. Cash had only just gotten home when they raided the place. He couldn't possibly have been in two places at once. He hadn't even dropped his bag on the ground when the DEA broke the door in. There wasn't time to stash anything. And there was nothing in his bag."

"Maybe it was already there."

"I just told you, I'd been there. There was nothing where they said they found it. I saw the police report. I made sure I went over it with a fine-tooth comb. The report is clean. They did everything by the book. It's like someone scripted the whole scene as a test to give new officers. But he's looking at getting locked away for life for something he didn't do."

She took a sip of her coffee, which had started to get cold, held both hands around the cup and stared at it.

"You don't believe me."

Tammie raised her gaze to him and shrugged. "I don't really know you or your brother at all. But I believe you believe he's innocent. I still don't know what this has to do with Serena."

"Because of the charges, and the fact that he traveled so extensively, the judge set bail at a cool million. My parents put their house up as collateral for the bail bondsman, and Cash was released. The last thing he said to me was that he was coming to Eastmeadow because Serena needed him. He'd never uttered her name before. He didn't tell me who she was or what she was to him. Just that he had to go. I've never seen him like that. No one has seen him since."

"I can understand now why you were so eager to talk to Serena."

He drained the rest of the coffee from his mug and set it down. "She knows something. She has to."

"Serena doesn't seem like she's in a condition to be much help. She was talking a lot of gibberish last night." She got up from the table. "Do you mind if I make another pot of coffee?"

"I could use another," he said. "Did you talk with her?"

As Tammie tossed the old coffee grounds and placed a new packet of coffee in the machine, she recalled the events in Serena's room.

"Not really," she finally said. "She was having a nightmare and was pretty out of it. It woke the whole house up. She kept crying over and over, 'They're stealing babies.'"

"Babies?"

"Yeah. It didn't make any sense." With the coffee-maker filled with water, Tammie hit the on button and sat back down.

"I'll admit I didn't expect her to be like that," Dylan said. "I didn't expect any of this." He said the last part quietly, looking out the window into the campground.

Some of the other campers were starting to rise, making their way out of tents and building fires.

"Do you think Cash skipped the country?"

"Cash? No way." He laughed, but it held no humor. "He's not the type to run from trouble. In fact, he's more the type to go straight into it with both guns cocked."

She raised an eyebrow, which he responded to by repeating, "He's not one to run from trouble."

"Did anyone see Cash here in town? I mean, if he came here to help Serena, someone might have."

"If they did, they're not talking."

Tammie thought of her parents, and the strange way they were behaving in the last months before their deaths. "Then what?"

He closed his eyes and took a slow, deep breath. "I'm afraid to even think sometimes, but it's hard. He was in trouble. And for someone to have it in for him enough to do the kind of damage they did, bringing in the drugs, making sure the DEA had him as a suspect, they'd have to be pretty heavily connected to organized crime. I hate even thinking of him caught up in that. It's the kind of thing he'd fought against in his job. I pray to the Lord every day to keep him safe, to watch over him and help him get out of whatever mess he's found himself in. Cash is a faithful man. He couldn't have done the things he's been accused of."

Tammie lifted her eyes to his. Something inside her warmed at the way he spoke of his brother and his unabashed way of speaking of his faith.

When she was growing up, talking about the Lord and her faith had been as easy as breathing in her house. Her parents had always said that God was the friend who was with you even when you were alone. She'd forgotten that over the past year. She never spoke of her faith to Bill. He wasn't a believer. He hadn't dismissed her when she talked about her faith, but soon she'd stopped talking about the Lord and how she felt His presence, because she knew it made him uncomfortable. Then she'd stopped talking about her faith altogether.

"What is it?" Dylan was looking at her, and she realized she'd drifted off in thought.

She felt her cheeks warm at having been caught day-dreaming. "It's just that it's nice to hear you talk about your faith. It's been a long time since I've been with someone who is that comfortable with it."

His brow furrowed. "You don't go to church?"

He wasn't accusing her, she realized. It was curiosity.

"I did. I stopped after my parents died. It's been hard." It pained her to say it. "My parents were very faithful people. They taught me that God was the one who sat in the empty chair next to you and then stood behind you when that chair was occupied by someone else."

He smiled. "That's a nice way of putting it. It's nice to think that wherever Cash is right now, God is with him."

"How do you think Serena is connected to Cash?"

"I think Cash was in love with her—is in love with her."

Her breath hitched. Had Dylan already given up hope that his brother was still alive?

"Yeah, I know," he said, misinterpreting her reaction. "But a relationship with Serena is the only thing I can figure. He never mentioned her at all. Not until the last day I saw him. It's like he was giving me a message that day. A riddle of some sort that he wanted me to figure out. Except I can't."

She shook her head. "It doesn't make sense. Why wouldn't he just tell you what was going on?"

"He said he was afraid for her. Said he had to get her out of here. The look on his face…"

"He never mentioned why?"

"No. I was so bowled over by the drug-trafficking charges and what to do about them—how to prove his innocence— that I didn't pay it much mention. I warned him about coming out to Eastmeadow, since he was on bail. He assured me it was going to be fine and that it was only going to be for a day or two." Dylan looked out onto the campground, regret etched in the lines of his face. "I should have come with him."

Dylan abruptly got up from the table and picked up his half-eaten plate of eggs. She hadn't done much better on her plate. He tossed his paper plate into the trash and stood by the camper door.

"What do you really think happened, Dylan?"

"I thought maybe Serena had something to do with it. But after meeting her, seeing how out of it she is, I think he stumbled into someone's territory and they didn't like it. He's not one to back away easily just because someone intimidated him. I know you're skeptical about his innocence."

"I didn't say that."

"You don't have to. I've read the expression you gave me many times. No one thinks he's innocent. But I know better. He never would have skipped bail to get out of punishment if he was due. And he never would have let my parents put their home up as collateral if there was a chance they'd lose it. Something happened to him that kept him from coming home. In my heart, I don't want to believe it, but I think he's… I think he's dead."

He turned to her then, and she saw the pain in his face at the thought that his beloved brother was gone. She knew that feeling all too well.

"You have a ray of hope I don't have," she said delicately.

"Meaning?"

Tammie wiped the toast crumbs from her hands onto her plate and then picked it up and tossed it in the trash along with the plastic-ware. She busied herself pouring another cup of coffee before turning around.

"You have hope of finding Cash. Maybe alive. I know it looks bad now. But you have to keep your faith that God will watch over him."

"Oh, I believe God is with him," Dylan said resolutely. "I just don't know where that is or what His plan is for Cash."

He stared at her for a moment, and awareness flashed across his face.

"You were talking about your parents when you said I have hope that you don't."

With the coffee cup in her hand, Tammie pushed through the camper door to the outside. A blast of fresh air hit her face, and she breathed deeply. She hadn't realized how claustrophobic she'd been feeling inside. Walking to her car, she leaned against it and took a sip of the hot liquid.

It took a minute, but Dylan followed her outside, holding a cup of freshly poured coffee in his hand. Tammie didn't look at him as he approached. Instead, she watched the people who were milling about. Some had towels draped over their shoulders as they headed toward the pond. Others were dressed in jogging clothes and were just out for a quick morning power walk. They nodded good morning as they walked by, but no one was really paying attention to them.

Dylan didn't say anything to her, as if he were giving her space to make up her mind about whether or not she wanted to talk.

"I don't remember telling you about my parents," she finally said.

"You didn't tell me directly. You mentioned to Aurore they were killed."

She closed her eyes. "Yes, in a boating accident, nearly two years ago."

"I'm sorry for your loss."

"Thank you. That's the reason I came here to Eastmeadow."

He frowned.

Her smile was weak. "We're not so different, you and I. You're searching for your brother and the truth about what happened to him. I'm trying to put my parents' deaths to rest by learning the truth about what really happened to them."

"You said they were killed in Oregon, didn't you?"

"Yes. But I think the answers lie here."

"Oregon and Massachusetts have a whole lot of country between them," he said.

"It's not like I put my finger on the map and decided to come here. I had my reasons."

"Care to share them?"

Something prickled inside her. She didn't need any more people shooting down her suspicions. She needed help. Dylan's interest in what she had to say was refreshing. After so many months of opposition from Bill and her other friends, to have someone believe that there might be something to what she'd suspected for a long time gave validation that she wasn't so crazy for coming all this way.

"After my parents were killed, I had the task of closing up their house in Winchester. I'd found a hatbox in my mother's closet. I'd seen it there before, but since it was among her private things, I never dared to look inside."

"Until she was gone."

Tammie nodded. "There were little mementos in there. A few birthday cards from my father, love notes, some pictures of my mother, me and my grandparents when I was a little girl. They'd died when I was quite young. And there was this letter from a person named Dutch. It came from Eastmeadow, and it mentioned closing their old house and taking care of things for them. And it said for them to stay safe. It was cryptic, to say the least, and it only had a post office box number."

Dylan thought a second. "Dutch. Was that a first or last name?"

"Don't know." She chuckled lightly. "There's a whole lot I don't know or understand about Eastmeadow or what happened, Dylan. I never even knew my parents lived here before. I've never seen a place that is so beautiful and yet holds so many secrets. Everyone that I've met here seems to have something to hide."

He darted his eyebrows up and made a face. "I get that."

"My parents weren't like that normally, though. At least, I'd never known them to be. So it seemed odd when for a few months before their deaths they acted…"

"Weird?"

"Exactly. I was so busy that I dismissed it. I was working and living on my own in Vancouver at the time, and hadn't been home in a few months. But then, all of a sudden, Dad called and insisted we go on a family vacation." Tammie snapped her fingers. "Just like that."

"What's strange about that?"

"This private cruise was like some urgent thing that had to happen *right then*. My mother called me every night to press me on it. They insisted I go with them."

She put the coffee mug on the hood of her car and turned around, leaning her elbows on the hood. "I finally agreed because I knew it was important to them. It was such short notice that I ended up having all these wild ideas that one of my parents was dying of cancer or something and wanted to go on one last family trip before they…"

She played with the dust on the hood of the car with her finger, making swirls and then wiping her fingers on her jeans.

"It was a nightmare getting the time off from work but I did it. The semester had just started at the private school I was working at, and because I wanted to get ahead and make sure my lesson plans were in place for the substitute teacher, I ended up being late to the marina."

"What happened?"

"I'd called my mother's cell phone to tell her I was going to be a little late. To save time, the captain decided to fuel the boat while they waited for me. The boat was at the fueling station when I got there."

She laughed without humor, shaking her head at the memory. "I remember looking at that boat, thinking my parents had to have spent their entire retirement to afford this stupid trip, and how angry I was that they did it. At the same time, I was scared out of my wits, because the only way I could figure my parents would do something so out of character was if someone was dying."

She dug her heel into the dirt, stared at a rock to keep control of her voice. "And then the boat just blew up."

"*What?*"

"Just like that. Flames and a million pieces all over the harbor. The boat exploded, and they were on it. My parents were killed, along with the captain."

Dylan blew out a quick breath. "I'm so sorry. It must have been horrible to see."

"Actually, I remember very little of the actual explosion. I was blown back into the water by the force of it, and was fished out by someone who'd seen the whole thing happen from the parking lot. If there hadn't been someone there who'd seen me go into the water, I would have drowned. The wind had been knocked out of my lungs. At first I couldn't breathe because of the force of the blast, and then later because I couldn't believe my eyes. Couldn't believe what had happened."

"You were lucky, then," Dylan said, placing his hand on her shoulder.

She shrugged. It hadn't felt that way when she woke up. Still didn't.

"What caused the explosion?"

"Officially? A fuel leak. But even the detective who investigated the explosion had his doubts."

"Why?"

"The boat my parents had chartered was a diesel. Diesel engines don't explode when taking on fuel, not like gas-powered engines. It takes a lot longer for the diesel fuel to fire. If there had been a leak, the captain would have recognized the signs, and they would have all been able to get off in time before it exploded. But they didn't. It just went up."

"Did the detective find any evidence the engine was tampered with?"

"There was no evidence to support it, even after a thorough investigation. But it was enough to cause suspicion."

His hands thrust into the pockets of his jeans, Dylan stood there, no more than three feet from her, just looking at her. "You would have been killed on that boat—"

"Yeah, if I hadn't been late. I would have been on that boat with my parents."

"The Lord was watching over you." He spoke the words as if he were trying to drive the point home.

She closed her eyes. "He spared me, and I've had a hard time accepting the reason why. Especially since…"

"Don't stop. Since what?"

She swallowed, trying to find the strength to put her thoughts in words. "Since I found out they weren't my biological parents."

His face registered surprise. "You mentioned that yesterday. Are you saying they never told you that you were adopted?"

"No," she added in a low voice. "I found out quite by accident a few weeks ago."

Admitting the truth out loud hadn't been as hard as she thought it would be. Until today, Tammie hadn't spoken a word about it to anyone except Bill. None of her other friends knew. She had no other family to speak of out west. Her aunt Betty had died a few years before her parents, and she'd barely known her grandparents. There was no one to call up and interrogate about why her parents had made the decision not to tell her.

But for some reason, it was easy to talk now. To Dylan.

"That's the reason I had to come here. It wasn't like them to keep a secret like that."

Tammie saw the compassion in Dylan's eyes, but before their gazes could hold for more than just a brief moment, he looked away.

"You do that a lot, you know," she said as he walked to the camper.

He opened the door, pulled out a half-full bag of trash and tied the ends into a knot. "Do what?"

"You're having a hard time looking at me. Don't try to deny it."

"Really? I wasn't aware of that."

She walked toward him. "Well, I am. Is it because when you look at me, you see Serena?"

SIX

Dylan was still holding the bag of garbage in his hand. He dropped it to the ground and gave Tammie his full attention.

"The resemblance is striking. I can't deny that it took me off guard yesterday. But why should that make a difference?"

Tammie folded her arms across her chest. "Because it's clear you blame Serena for Cash's disappearance."

She wasn't surprised that he didn't deny it. "I'll admit that for the month I've been in Eastmeadow, I've built up a fair amount of anger toward the woman, without having any reason, other than the fact that she has something to do with Cash's disappearance."

Tammie closed her eyes briefly, and sighed. His fear over his brother's disappearance must be overwhelming. Under the same circumstances, she might react the same way.

Still, she felt the need to defend Serena. "After meeting Serena yesterday, I wonder if she is as much a victim as Cash."

Dylan didn't look convinced. "Do you really believe that?"

Tammie sputtered. "Serena could hardly stand up on her own. Something is going on with her. And last night she was so incoherent. How could you blame her for anything that happened to Cash?"

His expression showed remorse. "Anger isn't an emotion I'm proud of. As you saw yesterday, I let my frustrations get the better of me sometimes. But I also know that any anger I have toward Serena is wasted energy. It'll only detract me from my real purpose here, and that is to find Cash. If it's His will, the Lord will help me find the right path to make it happen."

In that moment, Tammie realized what it was she found so appealing about Dylan. After all, given the way they'd met and the way he'd behaved, she had every reason to fear the man. And yet, even when he let his temper get the best of him, he quickly reined it in.

She envied the way he took control of himself. She wondered if it was his military training or his faith in the Lord that was at the core of it. Or maybe it was just Dylan. Even when he was full of frustration and anger, he had a sense of calm about him that radiated to her.

Looking around the campsite, Tammie realized it hadn't been that way for her. When her parents had been killed, she'd drifted farther and farther from the Lord. It just didn't seem possible that they'd been taken from her without reason. Deep down, she knew she'd been wrong to think that way. God was merciful. But no matter how hard she'd fought to let it go, she couldn't shake her feelings.

She'd always pictured herself with a faithful man in her life. Just like her father had been. Under different circumstances, she would have been attracted to Dylan. If they'd met on the street or at church, she would have allowed herself to act on the attraction she felt now.

She'd met Dylan under strange circumstances. How could she possibly entertain the thought of getting involved with a man like him, or any man, when she still had no clue about her past?

Besides, Cash was still missing; the only thing Dylan needed to focus on right now was finding his brother. And she needed to unravel the mystery of what had gone on all those years ago, when she was born. The last thing either of them needed was to distract themselves with the idea of romance.

It had only been twenty-four hours since they met, and he'd given her no indication of interest beyond what she could do to help him find his brother, she told herself. She didn't know the man. Those gazes he cast in her direction could mean anything.

She pushed the notion aside, feeling foolish that the thought had even entered her mind. There was more at stake here than what either of them *might* be feeling.

After clearing her throat, she said, "I think Serena was telling the truth yesterday."

"About what?"

"I think… I think I am her sister."

He gave her a crooked grin. "You're just figuring that out? I think it's obvious there's some family connection going on there."

"Aurore insisted that the baby Eleanor Davco was carrying died in the fire."

"She also pretended not to know you or your parents until you called her on it. She's lying. I think it's safe to say everything she tells you is suspect."

Tammie's head was throbbing. She placed a finger

against her temple to ease the pain. "I don't know when the fire was, but given the age Serena was in the picture, I'm guessing I'm only a year or two younger."

"I think you're right. How they could have missed a baby is beyond me. Someone must have questioned it. Surely your father…"

Her stomach coiled. It was hard to think of any man other than Aaron Gardner as her father. "Eleanor was pregnant. Maybe they didn't look for a baby."

"No reputable medical examiner would miss something like that. People must have known Eleanor was pregnant. The medical examiner would have questioned not finding the baby. If he didn't, he was paid off."

"Maybe people just assumed."

"More likely they didn't ask. And no one in this town is talking. At least not to me."

She closed her eyes as the sun poked above the line of trees and shone in her face.

When he spoke again, Dylan's face was sympathetic. "I'm going to get rid of that trash bag. I think there's still a cup or two left in the coffeepot. Why don't you polish it off, and I'll meet you inside, where the bright light won't bother you? You look tired."

Tammie nodded as he grabbed the trash bag and began to walk down the path toward the Dumpster. It wasn't fatigue that was dragging her down now. It was defeat. She'd come so far, and yet there was so much more she needed to know.

She grabbed her coffee mug, as well as the one Dylan had left on the picnic table, and went into the camper. The dregs of the coffee looked disgusting, so she turned off the power and drained the hot coffee down the sink. She was just rinsing out the pot when Dylan stepped into the camper.

"What about people who aren't from Eastmeadow?" she asked.

"You mean the auctioneers?"

"Yeah. From what the man at the motel said, there are a lot of out-of-towners that come here every year for the auctions. It's their livelihood. If they've been coming here long enough, they might have known the Davcos. Someone might remember what happened the night my— The night Eleanor died in the fire."

Tammie couldn't quite bring herself to say the word *mother* when referring to Eleanor Davco. In her heart, Connie Gardner would always be her mother.

"I'm sorry. You must be sick of listening to me go on about my parents when you have your brother to worry about."

"I think they're connected in some way."

Surprised, she said, "You do? But my parents lived here nearly thirty years ago."

"And took you with them to Oregon on the night that Serena Davco's mother died in a fire, leaving everyone to believe the baby she was carrying was killed, as well."

"What are you saying?"

"I don't know yet," Dylan said. "But I think it's time to clean up here and do a little antique shopping."

The auction grounds were littered with cardboard boxes and wooden crates cracked open to reveal their goods— everything from fine linens to china. The backs of flatbed trucks had furniture roped down—everything from dressing tables to armoires. The grounds ran along Main

Street, from the old white church on the hill and the stone-faced library, farther than Tammie could see. The streets were crowded with vendors hauling their wares off their trucks to display under tents.

With all the people milling about, and all the white tents popping up in fields that had been empty the day before, the scene reminded Tammie of a refugee camp. But no one was there to live. The auctioneers would only stay for the week and then pack their crates back onto their trucks and head to their next auctions.

"There have to be a few hundred dealers here," Dylan said, looking around.

"The motel clerk said they get somewhere in the neighborhood of seventeen-hundred dealers."

"By the looks of it, I'd say he's right."

Tammie blew out a quick breath, puffing her cheeks. "I don't know where to start. We can't talk to all of them."

"No, but we won't have to. Just concentrate on who's been around the longest. I'd say that's our best bet. Otherwise, we'll just be spinning our wheels."

Tammie pulled a small notebook out of her purse.

"What's that for?" Dylan asked.

"To take notes. You know, names, phone numbers…?"

He raised an eyebrow. "If anyone tells you anything important, you can get their card. If you walk around with a notebook, someone will think you're a reporter."

She hadn't thought of that. "Do you want to split up?"

"It makes sense. We'll cover more ground that way. Although it might be impossible to find each other after, since cell phone service is spotty in the center of town."

They walked a few minutes, looking at the workers

breaking open crates and lifting furniture onto the ground under the tents.

Tammie smiled, but didn't say much. Instead, she looked at their faces. Most of the men hauling boxes were young, maybe even still in high school. Some looked younger than the students in her class. Others didn't look much older than Dylan. She doubted any of them would have information to help her.

They found a tent where an older gentleman was setting up antique toys. On the table was a sign that read Fragile. In front of the sign was a red velvet cloth. On top of it was a fixed toy train with a metal frame.

"I think I had one of these when I was a kid," Dylan said, smiling. That got the owner's attention and he turned around and came over to them.

He was cordial when he spoke. "The fairgrounds don't open to the public until Tuesday. We get a hefty fine if we start dealing before then." He pulled a business card off the stack on the table and handed it to Dylan. "I'll be happy to help you if you want to come back then."

"We're not here to shop just yet," Dylan said, glancing at the business card before pocketing it. He glanced at Tammie and gave her an I-told-you-so smile. Tammie dropped her notebook back in her purse.

"Ah, it's a smart thing to scope out the goods ahead of time," he said, giving a wink to Tammie. "It's hard to move along these walkways when the crowds get here.

"That toy is twice is old as you are," the man said to Tammie. "I don't mind if you want to handle it. I don't let the kids. They all love to play with it, but it's too delicate a piece for little hands."

"It's beautiful," Tammie said, picking it up and turning it in her hand. She wasn't really interested in the toy train, but she had a feeling the dealer was flattered by the attention. "You must have people clamoring to get these pieces every year."

"I send out a mailing to the regulars. I don't have a Web site like some of the other dealers. Never did learn to use the Internet. I prefer selling face-to-face."

"Have you been coming here long?" Dylan asked. The seamless way he transitioned the question impressed her. She'd been walking past the tents, trying to figure out how to ask questions without looking like she was fishing for information. Dylan had her beat.

"Going on twenty years now."

She suppressed a sigh and smiled instead. "I imagine there aren't too many vendors who were here longer than you."

He laughed. "There are a few diehards who practically started the auctions. Old man Jackson started with a tent just like this, and now has that pretty building on the end of the strip open all year long."

"What about people from out of town?"

The man made a face like he was thinking. "John Beaumont and his people have been coming around for a while now. I'm pretty sure he was here before me. He sells all that antique china. I wouldn't want to be handling those pieces with a basket full of kids. Who ever heard of a gravy boat for eight hundred and fifty dollars?"

Tammie laughed at the comical face he made. "My, that's a bit out of my price range." The man had been working alone, and seemed to like the company. Part of her felt bad for fishing for information and moving on, but if he'd only been coming here for twenty years, he probably wouldn't have known her parents.

The man lowered his voice and leaned forward over the table. "Truth be known, some of these dealers will rob you blind. They're passing off reproductions at authentic prices."

"Really? Maybe we should stop by here for some advice before making any purchases," she said.

The man laughed and pointed a finger. "That's a wise thing to do."

Dylan had walked over to the next tent, and was talking to a man in his early twenties who looked as if he wanted to be anywhere but there.

"My friend has run off without me. Did you say John Beaumont has been here a while? Despite the prices, I do love good china."

"Yes, he's a few tent lanes down. Almost near the food court set up on the motel lawn. You can't miss him if you go round back here."

"Thanks. It was nice chatting. And good luck."

"Make sure you come on back on Tuesday," he said as Tammie walked away.

As she approached the next tent, she could hear Dylan talking to an older woman. The woman looked as if she was almost flirting with him, laughing and winking until Tammie walked up beside him. Then her expression collapsed.

"Well, now, who's this?" the woman asked.

"Tammie Gardner, I'd like you to meet Mrs. Trudie Burdett, owner of the Auction Acres."

Tammie extended her hand. "It's nice to meet you, Mrs. Burdett."

The woman nodded, her gaze holding steady to Tammie's face before she said, "Likewise. You can call me Trudie, dear. I feel so old when I hear my mother-in-law's name."

"Trudie has been selling her antiques in this very spot for over thirty years." He looked at her and raised his eyebrows, as if to say, now was her chance.

"Really? Then maybe you knew my parents."

"Knew? If they lived in Eastmeadow, I knew them. I know just about everyone in this town. If not by name, I know them by face. I never forget a face," she said, looking straight at Tammie.

"Aaron and Connie Gardner?"

Trudie shook her head. "Gardner? Can't say as I recall them."

Tammie popped open her purse and pulled out a picture of both of her parents that had been taken on Tammie's sixth birthday. If anyone were to recognize her parents, it would be easier with a photo that was taken closer to the time they lived in Eastmeadow.

But before she had a chance to show it to Trudie, the woman was off to the other side of the tent, yelling at the young man who was sitting on a sofa table.

"How many times have I told you not to stack the furniture that way, Maynard? If you get dirt on the finish, the price goes down."

"That's Maynard," Dylan said, smiling comically.

"I see."

Dylan lifted his hand to wave goodbye. "Trudie, it was a pleasure talking to you. Thanks for the information. And I'll be sure to stop by later."

Trudie turned and winked. "You do that."

Taking her by the arm, Dylan led Tammie in the opposite direction.

"But she didn't see the picture," Tammie protested.

"She doesn't have to."

"Why not?"

He stopped walking and looked at her. "Because she saw you." Then he continued walking down the lane.

Tammie had to walk fast to keep pace with Dylan's long strides. "I don't get it."

"Trudie Burdett practically started this antique fair. If she's been here for over thirty years—and she has—then she knows Serena Davco. She's not going to tell us anything."

"But I could have asked her about my parents. Maybe she doesn't remember their names, but if I'd shown her the picture—"

"Did you see the way she looked at you?"

"Yes."

Dylan shot her a quick grin. "She wouldn't have said a word."

"Why not? She seemed nice enough."

"She is. But she's still not going to tell us anything."

It seemed futile to argue with the man, but Tammie did anyway. Frustration building, she asked, "How do you know that?"

He stopped walking when they reached Main Street. With his hands on his hips, Dylan glanced up and down the street, as if he was looking for something in particular.

It amazed Tammie that the street looked nothing like it had yesterday when she arrived. Tents were set up deep into the fields, forming little villages.

Dylan seemed to find what he was looking for across the street and then led Tammie deeper into the marketplace. "I've asked Trudie about Cash probably ten times now. Different things each time," he finally said. "Each time, she changes the subject, and she never answers the question."

Tammie stopped short. "And starts flirting?"

He cast her a sidelong glance with a smile that could have lit up the sky. "I think she has a crush on me."

Tammie chuckled. "Oh, please…"

"What? You don't think so? You wound me."

Smirking, she said, "I have a feeling your ego can handle it. Okay, fine, Trudie Burdett is a bust. Now I need to go toward the motel, to talk to a man named John Beaumont."

"Who's John Beaumont?"

"Don't know. But when I was talking to the toy vendor, he mentioned that John Beaumont is from out of town and started working here before him. It's worth talking to him. And he's not a local. His tent is back toward the food court area."

"Then that's where we need to be."

They walked through crowds of workers carrying goods, being careful to sidestep anyone who couldn't see them. After asking a few people, they found Beaumont's tent.

John Beaumont looked younger than her parents had been, and Tammie immediately wondered if she'd reached another dead end.

"I started working here as a hand the year the auctions started. I hauled furniture just like these kids here," he said, pointing to the young men helping out. "You learn a lot if you pay attention, which I did until I was able to start my own business."

"Then you must remember that big fire at the Davco mansion," Dylan said.

"Fire?" Beaumont thought for a second. "Oh, you mean the big one up on the hill?"

"That must be the one," Dylan said.

Beaumont whistled. "I'd just about forgotten about that. It was a long time ago. Must be close to thirty years by now."

Tammie pressed him further. "Do you remember anything about it?"

The older man chuckled. "I remember it was big news back then. The details are a little sketchy, though. I do remember that the house was off the main road, but you could see that blaze light up the whole sky that night just like it was day. Seemed like the whole town was in the street looking at it. We were packing up that night and I remember we all stopped what we were doing, wondering what had happened. You could smell the smoke from that fire miles away...."

Tammie turned away. The picture Beaumont's words conjured up was too much to imagine. It had to have been horrible for those who lived through it.

Dylan seemed to sense her unrest. "Mr. Beaumont, do you remember what caused the fire?"

The old man drew in a deep breath and scratched his bald spot. "They'd been talking about that fire for weeks after it happened. I was still a young man, and didn't pay it too much attention beyond what people were talking about. I don't recall what started the fire, but with the fire, and the scandal with the pastor—"

"Scandal? What kind of scandal?" Tammie asked.

He pointed toward the center of town. "I'm talking about the pastor who used to serve at the white church on the hill here. I don't remember what the big deal was, but it was news at the time. Whatever it was, folks around here weren't too happy about what went down."

"Do you remember his name?" Dylan asked.

He shook his head. "It was a long time ago." Beaumont chuckled. "My memory isn't what it used to be."

Tammie pulled the photo of her parents out of her purse. "Have you ever seen these two people?" she asked.

Mr. Beaumont looked at the picture and shook his head. He pulled the picture back for another look when Tammie started to put it away, but then dismissed it.

"Like I said, it was a long time ago. I just don't recall all the details."

"Thank you for all your help."

"No problem."

It was hard for Tammie to squash her disappointment as they walked away from Mr. Beaumont's tent. It didn't seem possible that her parents had lived in this town, known these people, and never once mentioned it to her.

"I think you're right. We should split up," Dylan said.

"I thought you said we'd never find each other."

"We'll meet back at the library—say, in an hour?"

Tammie glanced at the rows and rows of tents laid out in the fields. "An hour isn't going to do much."

"Do you have another picture of your parents?"

"Yes." She took the other photo out of her purse and handed it to Dylan.

"You take one of Cash. We'll show them both, see what we come up with, then compare notes later. Maybe people will be more receptive to answering questions about Cash if you ask instead of me."

* * *

Dylan walked through the tent area, looking for anyone who might be old enough to have been in the area during the time when the Davco mansion caught fire. People were oblivious to his comings and goings, and that was okay by him. He didn't want to rouse suspicion that he was looking for information. Experience taught him that this was a town that liked to hold its secrets close.

He was just about to give up and walk back when he spotted two elderly men talking in the aisle.

"Excuse me," he said, interrupting them. "I was wondering if you could help me win an argument," he said to the gentlemen. "A female friend of mine says that this couple used to work here at the auctions some years ago, and I think she's wrong."

The men chuckled. "Leave it to a woman to get the facts all turned around," one of the men said.

Dylan couldn't help but chuckle himself. Not because the remark was funny, but because he was thinking of the reaction his kid sister would have if she heard a man utter a blanket statement like that about women.

"I've been living in this town my whole life," the other man said. "Let me see the picture."

Dylan showed the picture, and the man's smile changed to one of surprise, then recognition.

"Well, I'll be…" he said.

"You know them?"

"Sure do. Guess you lose the argument, young man. If I'm not mistaken, this is my old pastor and his wife."

Dylan blinked back his surprise. "Pastor?"

"Yeah, he and his wife… Can't remember their names

now, but they used to work the auction. Right there on the corner, across from the church." He pointed back toward the common area, where the library and the church stood. "They raised a lot of money one year selling donated items from the locals. Don't remember what the money was ear-marked for, but it left a bitter taste when the church money went missing."

"What do you mean, it went missing?"

"As in disappeared. No one could find the money. As far as I know, it was never recovered. Ended up being a big investigation. It was a shame they moved away, what with the scandal and all. The pastor was a likeable man. Always did like his sermons."

"Thanks," Dylan said, shaking the hands of both men. "Guess I owe the lady dinner."

The old man chuckled. "Sorry about that."

I am, too, Dylan thought as he walked away. If this man was correct, Tammie's parents had suddenly disappeared from Eastmeadow with a whole lot of secrets—and left a scandal in their wake.

SEVEN

Dylan didn't bother trying to get back to the library to meet Tammie. And he didn't have to check his watch to know whether they'd been walking around for an hour yet. He hadn't. But he figured Tammie would probably take every minute of that hour to flash those pictures around, so he went searching for her in the fields where they'd split up earlier.

She was determined to find the truth about her parents. He couldn't say that he blamed her for wanting to know. But he wondered if she'd truly considered what kind of truth she might find.

Probably not, he decided. And because of that, he'd keep the conversation with the old man to himself until he'd had a chance to check out whether or not it was fact. The last thing Dylan wanted to do was fill Tammie's head with information that proved to be unfounded.

Tammie's parents had supposedly lived here a long time ago. Memories fade, and people's recollections of events could easily become skewed over the years. The old man had provided the first bit of information that could lead Tammie to find out why she'd been taken to Oregon when her biological father and sister were still alive and living in Eastmeadow.

That meant two things. Tammie's parents had probably known her biological parents. And although Byron Davco might not remember who Tammie was now that he was in the nursing home, he'd known his biological daughter was still alive up until Alzheimer's took hold of him. Otherwise, why wouldn't Serena have been as shocked to see Tammie as she was to see Serena? She was too young to remember Tammie's birth. Someone must have told her about Tammie. And for sure, it hadn't been Aurore or Susan. The only person Dylan could think of was Byron Davco himself.

But why all the pretense? Children were put up for adoption all the time. If everything had been open and aboveboard, why wouldn't the Gardners have told Tammie she was adopted?

Dylan turned the conversation with the men around in his mind and wondered if Serena knew the reason. If she did, had she told Cash? Uncovering old secrets had a way of ruffling feathers.

If it weren't such a serious situation, Dylan would actually have laughed. Cash was better at ruffling feathers to get the truth than anyone he knew. He not only excelled at it, he took pleasure in it.

Cash's disappearance was somehow connected to Serena and to Tammie. Dylan was sure of it. The tough part would be figuring out how and why.

Traffic was still bumper-to-bumper when Dylan got to the street. He weaved in between a car and a truck filled with furniture and darted into one of the aisles, then back-tracked until he saw Tammie on a path deep into the field.

She was walking with John Beaumont, and she was laughing. Something Beaumont had said to her had her throwing her head back and placing her hand over her heart as if she couldn't breathe from laughing so hard. Dylan stood, rooted in place, just watching her face. She looked so carefree. He watched how the light from the sun brought out gold and red highlights in her dark hair.

Tammie was a pretty woman, with her shiny hair, high cheekbones and eyes that were lit up like fire. For a moment, the realization took Dylan off guard.

She cocked her head to one side and waved to Beaumont, then walked in the other direction away from Dylan. Trucks with furniture and crates lined both sides of the lane, making it difficult to pass. He didn't want to lose her in the crowd, so he sprinted.

"Tammie!" he called out to her. She turned around and stopped. She smiled when she saw him, her face like sunshine. What a change from this morning, when she'd been consumed with anxiety talking about her parents. It was as if just walking out into the fresh air and being with people had been enough to bring happiness back to her, help her forget how troubled she was.

Dylan was happy for her. And he hated thinking of how learning that her father had been the pastor involved in the town's scandal was going to distress her.

Tammie passed behind a large flatbed truck filled with crates. Maynard Burdett climbed into the back of it with a man Dylan didn't recognize. He did, however, recognize that Maynard was going to lengths to impress the man.

Dylan was only half paying attention to Maynard talking to the man. Instead, he watched as Tammie came around the other side. The two men lifted one of the crates into their arms and began to move it to the side of the truck. He couldn't see where they were placing it. What he could see was the large armoire teetering too close to the edge and the rope that was holding it in place suddenly snapping!

The armoire went down over the side of the flatbed truck and crashed to the ground on the other side, out of view. The two men struggled with the weight of the crate as the back of the flatbed wobbled. Then they lost the battle to hold on to their load. People ran toward the side of the truck that was hidden from Dylan.

"Tammie!" Dylan called out, running to where he'd last seen her. When he got there, he found her flat on her back on the ground. The armoire lay just inches from her, in pieces. The crate the men had been holding had broken open and emptied its contents at Tammie's feet. Dylan pushed through the crowd, his heart pounding in his chest, until he got to her.

The fear on her face was unmistakable. "It missed me." He wasn't sure if she was trying to reassure him or herself.

"Only by a split hair, child," Trudie said, running to Tammie's side.

The men on the back of the truck jumped to the ground. Dylan heard the truck's door slam as Maynard came around the corner to survey the damage.

With a deep scowl, the driver said, "Hey, someone is going to pay for this."

"It ain't gonna be me," Maynard said, looking at him.

Trudie scowled. "You almost flattened the girl, and you're worried about your paycheck?"

Maynard took in a harsh breath at his grandmother's words.

"Are you okay, sweetie?" Trudie asked Tammie.

"I'm fine," she said, but when Dylan took her by the arm to help her up, he felt her trembling. Or maybe it was him. His heart was racing faster than a locomotive.

"What happened here?" Trudie asked.

"It was an accident, Grandma," Maynard said.

"I don't care if it was an accident. I've just lost a crate of statues, and that armoire is over a hundred years old," the driver said.

As the driver and Maynard argued, two workmen struggled to pick up the armoire, now mangled and pulling apart, and carry it out of the aisle. Another man started picking up broken pieces of statues and separating them from the statues that had survived the fall.

The broken armoire and smashed clay told Dylan exactly what kind of damage Tammie had averted by jumping out of the way. She could have been seriously hurt—or worse.

Without thinking, Dylan brushed back the tangled hair that had fallen in front of Tammie's face. Her eyes were bright with fear, and the sight hit him like the blade of a knife. The need to protect her enveloped him.

"I'm fine," she said again, her eyes locking with his. It was then that he caught the slight tremor of her bottom lip. She quickly averted her gaze and gave her attention to the dirt on her hands. Dylan could tell she was anything but fine.

Voices arguing behind him pulled his attention away from Tammie.

"If you'd moved your truck quick enough, I could have unloaded my pieces myself," the man who'd been on the back of the truck was saying to Maynard.

Maynard Burdett threw up his hands and took a step back. "Hey, next time I won't offer to help."

"You call that helping?"

"It *wasn't* my *fault!* Who sits a piece of furniture on the edge of a truck like that, anyway?"

The driver pointed a finger at Maynard. "Those statues are worth more than you'll make this entire week."

Trudie was standing now, fists by her side. "Common courtesy says you should have waited until I unloaded my trucks before moving in, young man."

"I don't have all month, lady. The auction starts tomorrow."

"Don't you think we know that?" Maynard snapped.

Trudie huffed. "You two are a fine pair. You could have killed the girl, and all you're doing is worrying about your load."

"Good point, Trudie," Dylan said, holding Tammie's hand as he brought her to her feet. "Not one of you has asked how the lady is."

The driver of the truck glowered at them both. "I should be asking what you're doing nosing around these grounds, when only the dealers are allowed out here to set up. Accidents like this don't happen when—"

"I was just asking some questions," Tammie said.

The man looked at Tammie, his eyes cold. "If you don't want to get hurt, maybe you shouldn't go asking so many questions."

He got into the truck, fired the engine and drove the short distance to the next aisle. Dylan watched as he drove away, making note of where he was going—and the name on the side of the truck.

Aztec Corporation. He'd seen that name before, but for the life of him he couldn't figure out where.

The truck took a right turn, heading back toward the

street. *Interesting,* Dylan thought. The man still hadn't finished unloading his crates.

The only piece of furniture the truck had held was that armoire. Strange. Making a mental note to look into the vendor's tent later, he turned his attention to Tammie.

"My jeans are wrecked," she said with a shrug and a quick smile. Her knee was visible through the tear in the denim.

"Does it hurt?" he asked.

"My knee? It'll be fine."

Answering the worried look he knew was on his face, Tammie rolled her eyes and smiled. "If I said I had a hangnail, would that make you happy?"

He brushed his fingers down her cheek. "No. I don't want you hurt at all."

Her gaze met his and held it for a long moment. "Too late," she said.

His face must have shown panic, because Tammie quickly added, "I'm only talking about my ego. It wasn't a very ladylike fall, if you know what I mean."

Trudie burst out laughing. "You can't be graceful *and* make a quick getaway, dear."

Dylan chuckled at that, more out of nervous energy than anything else.

Trudie touched Tammie's shoulder. "You best be going home to check that knee out."

"Thank you, Trudie," Tammie said. "You're right."

Dylan could tell Tammie was still rattled as they silently walked back to the church parking lot where he'd parked his Jeep.

"You look as though you've got a lot spinning in your

head," she finally said as they reached the Jeep. "Did you find anything out?"

Dylan glanced up at the big white church and thought about telling Tammie what the old man had said about Aaron Gardner being the pastor here years ago.

"You don't think that was an accident back there, do you?" Tammie said, settling in the passenger seat.

"Why do you say that?"

"You've been quiet ever since we left the auction grounds."

It was true that Dylan was wondering if what had happened was truly an accident. The fact that there was one lone piece of furniture on a truck filled with statues didn't quite sit right with him. But then, what did he know about antiques or auctions? Maybe all the vendors had an odd assortment of things to peddle.

He'd call Sonny tonight and have her check out Aztec Corp. For some reason, it rang a bell with him, and maybe his sister would know why. While he was at it, he'd check in with his partner, Matt, to see if he could find out anything on Aurore and Susan. Although the Captain made it clear that Dylan wasn't to use department resources to gather information about the possible whereabouts of his brother, Dylan knew Matt was eager to help. He'd only use him for information he knew Sonny couldn't find herself.

"I'm just tired from all the talking," he finally said.

The way the driver of the truck had looked at Tammie, it had almost been as if he blamed her for the lost load. But Dylan had no proof that what had happened was anything but an accident. And because of that, he was content to let Tammie think it was—at least for the moment.

When he had a better understanding of why that truck

had been down that lane, he'd share his suspicions with her. For now, he just needed to get her back to the mansion so that he could do a little investigating on his own.

"Where have you been all day?"

Aurore's glare said much more than words ever could, Tammie thought as she walked up the walkway toward the mansion's door. She and Dylan had debated whether to take the time to go back to the campground to get Tammie's car or come straight to the mansion. They both wanted a chance to talk to Serena, so Tammie had suggested they get her car so that Dylan could talk to her first and then leave to do the errands he'd mentioned to her.

He'd been preoccupied when they left the auction grounds. Maybe he was just tired, as he'd said. Fatigue was wearing her down, too.

Tammie took in Aurore's hard scowl as they approached the front door.

Kill her with kindness, she thought. Not that Tammie believed it would make a difference. "I went out early and didn't want to disturb anyone," she said.

Aurore looked past Tammie, to Dylan. "I should have known she was with you."

"Nice to see you again, too, Aurore," Dylan said, pasting a smile on his face. "Miss me?"

Aurore's hands knotted. Ignoring Dylan, she turned to Tammie. "Next time you leave the house at the crack of dawn and are gone all day, at least have the courtesy to tell me."

Tammie was speechless.

"Do you always keep such close tabs on your house-guests?" Dylan asked.

Aurore sighed. "I'd rather not have to run through the house looking for people. I have enough work to do here."

Tammie glanced at Dylan's suspicious face and then back at Aurore. "It was so early, I didn't want to wake anyone. I'm sorry. I should have left a note."

Aurore nodded, and her expression changed to one of resignation. "Serena was calling for you."

"Is she still in her—"

"Sleeping. I gave her a sedative. She was quite upset you weren't here when she woke up. She thought you'd left for good. I assured her your bags were still in your room."

"I'll go see her, then," Tammie said as she and Dylan walked into the house.

Aurore's hand held her back. "No. I told you, I gave her a sedative. She hasn't had her dinner yet and I was getting ready to bring it to her as soon as she wakes up."

Tammie sighed. Were they ever going to get a chance to talk to Serena?

Susan came into the room. She was about to say something to Aurore, but stopped short when she looked at the tear in Tammie's jeans. "Do you know your leg is bleeding?"

Aurore's expression suddenly shifted to one of concern. Reaching down, she opened the gap at Tammie's knee. "You *are* bleeding. What happened to you?"

Tammie inspected her knee. "I didn't notice. I thought it was just a scrape."

"What did you do to her?" Aurore asked Dylan accusingly.

"Nothing," Dylan told her. "A load of furniture fell off a truck while we were at the auction grounds. It nearly hit her."

Aurore gasped. "What were you doing down there?"

"Shopping," Dylan said dryly. Walking over to the table by the sofa, he picked up a small statue. "Nice piece. I saw something similar to this in one of the tents."

"Put that down," Susan demanded.

"Susan," Aurore said, "why don't you see to Serena's dinner? She may be awake soon. I'm sure she'll be hungry."

Susan did as she was told. It was clear she wasn't going to cross Aurore.

"I'm sorry," Aurore said to Dylan. "Susan can be a little protective. In the future, I would appreciate it if you asked before you touched anything."

She took the statue from Dylan's hand and placed it back on the sofa table, then turned to face them.

Tammie thought it odd. It was only a statue. Perhaps it held sentimental value.

She knew nothing of this house or the people who occupied it. Although evidently connected by blood, she was as much an outsider here as Dylan.

"I don't like the idea of you going down to the auction grounds," Aurore said. "It's not safe."

Tammie smiled warmly at the sudden concern on Aurore's face. "I was with Dylan."

"Exactly."

Dylan rolled his eyes. "It sounds like Serena will be asleep for a while, so I'm going to go. Will you be okay?" he asked Tammie.

Aurore's mouth dropped open. "Of course she'll be all right, now that she's home."

"Home? I seem to remember you calling her some pretty harsh names yesterday."

At Aurore's puzzled look, Dylan added, "'Imposter'?"

She lifted her chin. "You were leaving?"

"Yes," he said, and it seemed to satisfy Aurore to some degree. "I have some errands."

Tammie squashed her disappointment. Dylan had been more than helpful to her today. She couldn't monopolize all his time, when he had his own search to continue. Still, she'd enjoyed the day more than she'd thought she could. More than she remembered enjoying any day in a long time.

His eyes held a warmth that touched her. "I'll be by tomorrow," he told her, then turned to Aurore. "Early. Just so you can expect me."

"I'll be counting the hours until you return," Aurore said sarcastically, then turned on her heel and stalked out of the room, toward the kitchen.

Dylan waggled his brows. "I think she's starting to like me, don't you think?"

Tammie couldn't help but laugh. "If it weren't so strange, it'd be funny."

"Well, she is a bit odd."

"She's hiding something."

"You think?" He eyed her, and she smiled, surprised to find that she could. "Whatever it is, I'm dying to find out."

"She seemed almost afraid for me," Tammie said, recalling her expression when she learned they'd been at the auction grounds.

"Concerned, or annoyed?"

"Are you always this suspicious of people's intentions?"

Dylan blew out a quick breath. "Lately, I'm afraid I am."

"Well," she said, "I guess it's not as if you don't have a good reason."

"Thanks for understanding. And…for this morning."

Puzzled, she asked, "What about this morning?"

"For not judging Cash. For at least being willing to see things another way. It was refreshing."

Tammie shrugged slightly. "Everyone deserves a chance to prove themselves." She thought about her parents, and how they weren't going to have the chance to tell her why they hadn't told her the truth.

She rubbed her temple.

"Another headache?" Dylan asked.

She nodded. "And I'm exhausted. I think jet lag has finally taken its toll. But I'm going to try to talk to Serena tonight. Hopefully alone."

"You have my cell phone number handy. Unlike in the center of town, I get a pretty good signal at the campground, so you shouldn't have any trouble getting through to me if you need to call."

"Thank you, too. For everything *you* did today."

He nodded. "Try to get some rest." With his hand on the doorknob, he added, "Oh, and make sure you use the lock on your bedroom door."

Tammie doubted she'd be able to sleep. Her schedule was so off-kilter, she didn't know whether the sun was setting or rising. She was thankful Susan wasn't around to give her a hard time. After having so little sleep the night before, she felt as if she could slide into bed and sleep for a hundred years.

She climbed the stairs, taking a long look at the painting on the wall. The swell of Eleanor's stomach was the only evidence that Tammie had been part of this family. It was odd that she had chosen to have the painting done before

Tammie was born. Why wouldn't she have wanted both children in the picture?

She sighed, climbed the rest of the stairs and made her way to her room.

The setting sun filled the room with an amber glow. Tammie flicked the light switch to find her way around the room without knocking into things.

The bed was still unmade. It looked inviting, with its rumpled blanket and sheets and the pillow that still had the imprint of her head on it. Sitting down on it, she flipped her sneakers off and reached into her jacket pocket to pull out her cell phone.

She'd turned it off earlier, not wanting to be disturbed by calls from well-meaning friends. Well, *one* well-meaning friend in particular. Now she heard the familiar *bing* that indicated she had a message.

No, she thought, glancing at the screen. *Voice mail messages.*

"Bill, you are relentless," she muttered with a chuckle.

Pressing the button to connect to her voice mail, she slipped off her socks and rubbed her feet as she waited for the automated voice to play.

"You have four new messages," it announced.

She didn't bother listening to them. Instead, she dialed Bill's number from memory and waited for him to pick up.

"I knew you'd answer on the first ring," she said. *Predictable and steady.*

"You didn't call last night," Bill said accusingly. It wasn't like him to be this demanding, but he must have been worried.

"It was late." A twinge of guilt crept into Tammie's voice.

"Not for me. I'm on the other side of the United States. I would have been up. And I *was* up. Do you know why? Because I was waiting for you to call."

"Sorry."

He sighed. "So are you ready to come home yet?"

"No," she said quickly. "I just got here."

This was not a conversation she was going to let him drag her into again, about how she was being paranoid. He'd spent last week trying to convince her that she should stay in Winchester and beg the dean's forgiveness for her abrupt departure and ask for her job back.

"I'm working with someone here," she said, getting right to the point.

Silence.

"Bill?"

"Who?"

Okay, that meant he was listening. "A man name Dylan Montgomery. He's a police officer from Chicago."

"He's a long way from home, then."

She gave his comment a quick chuckle. "He's looking for his brother."

"What does that have to do with you?"

She closed her eyes. The truth was, she didn't know if it had anything at all to do with her. The only connection they had was Serena.

"I'm not sure yet. But he thinks we can help each other."

"I don't like it. He could be some nutcase trying to take advantage of you."

She smiled, remembering how Dylan had stepped in front of her car on the street. She'd thought he was crazy then.

"He's a nice guy. Decent. You'd like him." No, he

wouldn't. Dylan and Bill were about as different as two people could be.

"Really?" Bill didn't sound convinced. "You've got a thing for him?"

"I just got here, Bill." She rolled her eyes, but something inside made her feel like she wasn't being completely aboveboard with her friend.

"Hey, I've known you since we were in junior high school. I know when you have a crush on a guy."

"What are we, in seventh grade again? No, I do not have a crush," she said.

"Yeah, you do. You just don't know it yet."

"How do you know that?"

"I know because it was never me."

Tammie didn't have a quick comeback for that. She'd always known that Bill wanted more from their friendship than what they had. But while she enjoyed, even treasured their friendship, she simply couldn't get seriously involved with a man who didn't share her faith in the Lord.

"I don't have a crush on anyone." She said it as delicately as she could. "I'm too busy for that."

"How'd you meet this guy?"

She arched an eyebrow. Did she really want to go there? "Dylan is just a guy looking for his brother, and he's helping me find out some things about my parents."

That much was true. She hoped it was enough to satisfy Bill's curiosity.

"So?"

"So, what?" she answered.

"Has he? Helped you find out anything about your mom and dad?"

Tammie quickly filled him in on the few things that had happened since she'd arrived in Eastmeadow, leaving out the part about how she'd actually thought Dylan was *crazy* when she first met him. To Bill's credit, despite his reservations about her staying at the mansion, he didn't press her.

"Don't make me call you fifty times before you answer," he said, his voice filled with concern.

Tears welled up in her eyes. "I won't. I'm sorry I made you worry. I'm on to something. I was right to come here."

"I miss you," he said quietly.

She sighed softly. "I'm sorry about that, too, Bill. I'll talk to you soon."

Tammie had known Bill a long time. Of all her friends, he was the one who could read her the best. That was why he'd known she needed to go back to Winchester after her parents' death. It was also why he'd known that once she found out about the DNA tests, she wouldn't be able to let it go.

And why he'd known that Dylan was something more than just a man helping her search for the truth. But even Tammie didn't have the answer to what that something was.

EIGHT

"Guess what, Dyl?" Sonny said to him over the phone as he put together a peanut butter and jelly sandwich.

"What?"

"Aztec Corporation makes statues."

He dropped the knife on the paper plate and waited. When she didn't elaborate, he heaved a heavy sigh that got her attention.

"I already knew that, Sonny. I saw about a half dozen of them smashed on the ground." *And one in the Davco mansion.*

"Oh."

"That's it? That's all you could find?"

Sonny was good at research. If there was a way to uncover information about Aztec Corporation, she'd do it.

"That's all there was on the surface," Sonny said, a little hint of satisfaction in her voice.

He rolled his eyes. "What's under the surface, Son? Don't keep me in suspense."

She chuckled. She was having fun with this. Most of the time, her job as a computer-software specialist was rather dry, she'd told him. She worked at a high-tech company, figuring out ways to hack into systems and keep others from doing the same. She was good at what she did.

"I'm not asking for you to do anything illegal."

"I know you're not. And you know I wouldn't. Even if I could." And she probably could, Dylan thought. "There just isn't a whole lot out there. Nothing beyond suspicions, and the fact that Aztec Corporation is far from home."

He'd just picked up his sandwich to take a bite, but he dropped it back on the plate, curious about where she was going. "Go on."

"The Aztec Indians were not South American. They were Mexican. Yet the headquarters for Aztec Corporation is in Colombia."

"Haven't you ever seen Native American dolls that were made in China?"

She paused, then said, "You've got a point."

"Yeah, give me something else."

"I'm just wondering, why not sell statues of their own culture? Colombian art is beautiful. So I looked it up."

"And?"

"Aztec Corporation sells fakes. Bad fakes. As in completely wrong."

"That's a great art-history lesson, sis, but I need something to go on here. When I saw the name on the truck, it was as if I'd seen it before."

"You think Cash was investigating it?"

"Don't know. He never said anything."

"Same here."

"Is that all you have?"

"Pretty much. There was some press about some paintings that were stolen like a million years ago."

"How long?"

"Um, hold on." She paused, as if she were checking the computer. He heard the clicking of keys. "Looks like they were stolen almost thirty years ago, but one of them just popped up on the black market a while back. Do you think that's something?"

"I don't have a clue. But if it has to do with Aztec Corporation, check it out."

"I can comb Cash's apartment tonight to see if I can find that info he had on Aztec Corporation if you want. Maybe he has something there that I can use to look into this a little deeper."

Dylan thought about it. He could easily have missed something when he searched the apartment before he left. "Take Dad with you."

She sighed heavily. "I'm not twelve, Dylan. I can go to my own brother's apartment and water the plants—which, by the way, are dying."

He laughed. "You forgot to water them."

"I watered them too much, I think. You know I don't exactly have a green thumb."

"Have Mom nurse the plants back to health. If that doesn't work, we'll get Cash a spider plant. He'll never know the difference."

"Yeah, he will. He notices everything. And he'll blame me."

Dylan liked talking about their brother as if he was still part of the here and now. It was too upsetting to think of the alternative.

His appetite suddenly gone, he pushed the plate with the sandwich away. "E-mail me when you have something, okay?"

Sonny promised to do that, then hung up. Dylan put the cell phone on the table and scrubbed his hand over his face as he looked out into the darkness. Most of the campers had doused their campfires and turned in.

He should be doing something. He didn't want to lie in bed, waiting for the hours to pass until he could go back to the Davco mansion and talk to Serena.

Yeah, right, that's the reason, he said to himself as he got up from the table and pushed the camper door open. The warm night air bathed his face. The days were getting hotter. Summer was here.

He hoped he hadn't sent Sonny on a wild-goose chase. Aztec Corporation might just be another company trying to make a buck by copying and selling pottery originally made by ancient civilizations.

Looking up at the moon, he closed his eyes and said a prayer to the Lord.

"I know I've been asking a lot lately, Lord. And You've given me the direction I need. I just want to say thanks for leading me here."

And for leading me to Tammie. He didn't say that part out loud, but Dylan knew He understood.

"Let me take the tray to her," Tammie said, holding out her hands.

Susan stood at the foot of the stairs, a dinner tray filled with food in her hands. Serena's dinner was being served at nine-thirty, because she'd slept so late.

"It's my job. I'd appreciate your letting me do it."

Tammie put her hands down. "Fine. Then I'll go with you. I'd like to see how Serena is doing."

"That won't be necessary. Aurore is already up there."

Despite the attempted brush-off, Tammie followed Susan up the stairs and into Serena's room. She didn't know what to expect after last night's nightmare. Serena had been distraught the night before, but Tammie was caught off guard when she found that she was worse.

Serena lay lifeless in her bed. Aurore stood next to her, lifting her so that she was sitting almost upright, propping her up with pillows. Her eyes were glazed over, and she appeared almost catatonic, with her head slightly turned to the side.

Aurore turned as Tammie came beside the bed. "You might want to get some dinner yourself, since you didn't eat when you got home," Aurore said to Tammie. "Susan is a good cook. She'll fix you something."

"Thank you, but I had dinner earlier, in town."

Aurore sighed. "As you can see, Serena is not up to talking. You'll be wasting your time if you try."

"Isn't that for me to decide?"

"Why don't you find something else to do?"

"You're trying to get rid of me again," Tammie said pointedly.

Aurore gave her a half smile. "Would it work if I were?"

"No."

"Then it'll only be a waste of my time if I try."

Susan put the dinner tray on the space at the foot of the bed, and Aurore cleared a spot there and sat down. "That will be all, Susan. Thank you."

When she was gone, Tammie pulled a chair closer to the bed, opposite where Aurore was sitting.

"Did you raise her?" she asked.

Aurore gave her attention to feeding Serena. "Serena? No, her father did."

"A mother's love is important, too. She had no step-mother?"

"Eleanor was her mother. I made sure she knew what kind of woman her mother was. Her father never remarried."

An ache settled in the pit of Tammie's stomach. She knew nothing about any of them. Would she have the opportunity to know what kind of person Eleanor Davco had been, and how she had come to live in someone else's home? She hoped so.

"You'll have to tell me about that sometime. If you don't mind."

Aurore's face remained expressionless, but she paused for just a fraction of a second before she continued to spoon-feed Serena.

Food dribbled out of Serena's mouth, and Aurore quickly scooped it away from her face and wiped her with a soft white cloth, as if she were a baby again. The scene was almost too much for Tammie to bear.

"What's wrong with her?"

"She hasn't gotten over the loss of her father."

"He's in a nursing home. He's not dead."

"He is to Serena. He doesn't remember her at all. It was a devastating blow to be left alone like that."

But she's *not* alone, Tammie wanted to say. More and more, she was becoming convinced that she was Serena's sister. How could they be so alike and not be sisters? It just didn't make sense.

"She wasn't always like this?"

Aurore tried to spoon some food into Serena's mouth, coaxing her. "Off and on. She's suffered from mental illness throughout her life. First the trauma of losing her mother in the fire, and then losing her father."

From where Tammie was sitting, she had a clear view of Aurore's scar. "Did you get that way in the fire here at the mansion?"

Aurore turned to her, startled. Then her face changed. Tammie had expected anger, but she saw none. What she saw instead was more a look of surprise.

"You sure are a curious one," Aurore finally said.

Tammie closed her eyes, guilt eating at her. "I'm sorry if I offended you."

She was surprised when Aurore chuckled.

"No, you're not. You're curious. I can see the questions behind your eyes, and I know that you're having a hard time keeping yourself quiet. You want to know everything."

Tammie asked, "Is that so wrong, given the circumstances?"

Aurore seemed to weigh her words. "You want to know about this ugly scar? I've been with the Davco family since before Serena was born. I was here the night Eleanor Davco died. I tried to help her, but failed. And I'll tell you one more thing—you shouldn't be asking so many questions."

"Why not?"

Aurore dropped the spoon in the half-empty dish. "People get hurt when they ask too many questions."

"I'm not trying to cause—"

"Trouble? Well, you are. More than you know. If you don't want trouble to find you, then you need to leave it alone. If you can't do that, I suggest you pack your bags and go back home to Oregon."

Tammie lifted her chin, glanced at Serena, heard a soft moan escape her lips, as if she were trying to communicate with them.

Tears stung Tammie's eyes, but she wouldn't let them show. She wouldn't let Aurore know how much her words had hurt. If her parents hadn't left Eastmeadow, she would have grown up in this town, just like Serena. As hard as it still was for her to imagine, she probably would have grown up right here in this house.

Dylan had told her to keep her faith. But it was becoming harder and harder to cling to the belief that her parents hadn't known she was not their biological child. They must have known. If they really had lived in Eastmeadow, they would have seen Tammie's resemblance to Eleanor Davco. Maybe not at first, when she was a baby, but certainly when she grew up.

"No one is going to force me away from here," Tammie said quietly, "no matter what questions I ask."

Rising from her chair, she gave a gentle squeeze to Serena's hand, but got no response. *Oh, Serena, please wake up and talk to me.* How could she possibly get answers to all the questions burning in her mind without the aid of her sister?

It was selfish of her to think only of herself, when Serena so clearly was the person in need. But until she could talk to Serena and find out what she knew about Tammie, how she'd known Tammie was coming, and what all this had to do with her parents, she just couldn't move on.

She left the room and shut the door. This house didn't feel like a home. It was a fortress. She was free to leave, but how could she leave with Serena here, without knowing how her life had come to be what it had?

Her mind wandered to Dylan. He'd said he had some things to take care of tonight, but she wished he was still here with her. Aside from Serena, he seemed to be the only ally she had in a town that held too many secrets.

He'd taken her arm earlier, held it in a way that made her feel protected. It was almost as if she could still feel his touch. Her adrenaline raced at the thought of what could have happened at the auction grounds today, had she not been able to get out of the way of the falling armoire. She'd never been so scared in her life. And she'd never been so glad to see anyone as she had been when Dylan suddenly appeared by her side.

She touched her knee and winced at its tenderness. It would feel a little achy for a few days. She'd had a chance to clean out the scrape and seen the nasty bruise that had already turned purple and swollen.

Dylan was convinced the armoire had been a warning. She couldn't say she was completely convinced herself, but she would make sure the door to her bedroom was locked.

NINE

The moon was sitting behind thick clouds, making it impossible to see anything without strong headlights or a flashlight. Dylan's eyes were good, though. He'd been on many ops where the moonlight, although pretty, was his team's downfall, making it harder to search for what they were looking for.

Or to remain unseen by those he didn't want to know he was there.

Tammie had said there had been someone lurking in the garden last night. It had frightened her, and Dylan couldn't say he liked the idea of it, either. After today's near miss at the auction grounds, he wasn't going to leave it to chance that it wouldn't happen again.

When he'd seen her splayed out in the dirt, he couldn't breathe until he saw her moving. Then he'd held her in his arms, felt her heart beating as strongly as his own and known she was all right.

Although there was no proof, he saw the accident as a message of some kind. Whether it was from someone at Aztec Corporation or if they were merely the messengers, he didn't know. What he did know was that someone wasn't happy they were asking questions.

And he didn't want Tammie to get caught in the crossfire. She had her own reasons for being here. He didn't know what had made the pastor and his wife take her from Eastmeadow and move clear across the country without anyone knowing about it. Or why they'd kept the fact that she had a whole family in Eastmeadow a secret from her all these years.

But Dylan was sure that it was all connected with the reason Cash had disappeared. He was waiting for Sonny to e-mail him with the information he'd asked her about earlier. If his suspicions were right, he'd have his first lead about Cash's disappearance since he'd gotten to Eastmeadow.

He'd parked the car down the road a ways, so as not to rouse the suspicions of anyone in the house. Tall maples lined the street and stretched over the road, keeping the moonlight from revealing his presence.

Eastmeadow was so unlike the streets he worked as a cop. Unlike here, he knew what kind of trouble lurked in the shadows in a big city. He'd have to draw on his years in the Marines tonight. He was used to dealing with all kinds of situations, changing course on the fly, and moving unnoticed until he was ready to reveal himself. If there was someone out here tonight, he'd find him.

Keeping his breathing steady, Dylan moved slowly around an overgrown arborvitae to the back of the house. It was nearly midnight, and the windows on the second floor of the mansion were dark.

He sat at the edge of the woods, watching the moon move across the sky for another hour or so. The wild animals were on the prowl for food. A large wood owl hooted and screeched high in a tall pine tree behind him, letting Dylan know he didn't like the intrusion in his world. Dylan stayed anyway, and eventually the owl flew away.

It was nearly two-thirty when he heard someone digging in the side yard. Dylan moved toward the sound. Someone was crouched down on the ground as he approached. If it was a man, he was slight of build, but Dylan wouldn't underestimate his strength by his size. He crept up behind him.

"Stand up and turn around slowly. I want your hands where I can see them."

The only weapon Dylan had was a tree branch he'd cleaned off while he was looking around earlier. But he could use it to defend himself, if need be.

The man rose slowly from the ground.

"Whatever you have in your hand, drop it!" Dylan said, his voice commanding.

Something fell to the ground. "It's just a spade," the man said. "I don't have a weapon. Just garden tools. Don't hurt me."

Dylan kept his distance from the man. He picked up the item the man had dropped to the ground. It was *indeed* a small garden spade. "What are you doing out here?"

"I work here."

"Nice try. Want to give me another? This time, something believable."

"It's true. Ask Aurore. I've worked here since before Mr. Davco was taken to the nursing home. Going on ten years now."

Dylan took a step closer. "If you work here, what are you doing out in the yard in the middle of the night?"

"I always work at night. I can't take the sun, and the mosquitoes aren't as bad this time of night."

"Just what do you do?"

"I'm the Davcos' gardener."

"Gardener, huh? Doesn't look like you're doing such a hot job, by the looks of it during the day."

The man shrugged. "I do my best. They have a limited budget, you know?"

"Right."

"Are you a cop or something?"

Dylan eyed him. The *something* part was right. He was a cop, although he wasn't here in any official capacity. "I don't think you're in a position to be asking me questions, when you were the one caught out here."

"I'm telling you the truth. I have nothing to hide. Just ask the staff here."

"What's your name?"

"Sam. Sam Watson. I live over in the next town." Sam had his hands in the air and was starting to shake. "Ask Aurore. She'll tell you. I've been working here for years."

"Okay, Sam Watson. Why don't we do just that?"

Aurore stood in the foyer, staring at Dylan and Sam in the doorway. "Was it necessary to wake up the *whole* house for this?"

Out of the corner of his eye, Dylan saw Tammie coming down the stairs, wrapped in a blue terry bathrobe.

"What's going on?" she asked. Then her eyes widened when she saw Sam Watson.

"He claims he's your gardener."

"He doesn't claim anything," Aurore said with an impatient sigh. "He *is* the gardener. This is why you felt the need to wake us all up?"

"What is he doing out in the yard at this time of the night?" Dylan asked.

"He prefers to work that way. Mr. Davco approved of it, and I didn't see any reason to change things once Mr. Davco was no longer here. The way I see it, you're the intruder. Not Sam."

"You're the man I saw in the garden last night," Tammie said, coming into the foyer and addressing the gardener.

"I didn't know anyone saw me. I thought everyone was asleep. I don't usually wake anyone when I'm working."

"You're sure this is the man you saw?" Dylan asked.

Tammie nodded.

"Sam has been a loyal employee for years. I sometimes make him breakfast before he goes home."

Dylan pushed aside the weirdness of this arrangement. "Has he ever taken anything from you?"

Aurore's eyes flared with fire. "You mean steal? Never!"

"Check his pocket," Dylan said.

"No, I will not."

"Sam, are you going to come clean about the noise your pocket was making as we walked to the front door? Now, I'm not real good at the sounds a garden spade makes when it's shoved in a pocket, but I did see you stuff something in there, and it made an awful racket rubbing up against something else. How about it?"

"What are you talking about?" Looking at Sam, Aurore asked, "Sam, what is going on?"

The remorse on the gardener's face said it all. He pulled out the contents of his pocket and held them in his hands for everyone to see. Wide-eyed, Aurore picked through the tangle of chains and rings and found a diamond pendant and necklace encrusted with dirt from being buried in the ground. A ring was tangled in the chain of the necklace and wouldn't pull free. Aurore spread the jewelry out in the palm of her hand and examined it.

"Why, these were Eleanor's. They were lost in the fire," Aurore said, moving the pieces in her hand and brushing away dirt.

"Are you sure?" Tammie asked.

"Of course I'm sure."

"You want to explain how you came by these?" Dylan said.

The hurt on Aurore's face was unmistakable. "Sam, I don't understand. How did you get these? How could you have these?"

Sam hung his head.

Tammie looked at the pieces of jewelry in Aurore's hand. One of the rings had a large stone, but Tammie couldn't make out what it was. "How can you tell they are the same pieces of jewelry?"

"Eleanor had a lot of jewelry. Mr. Davco was very generous that way, as was her father. But most of it was lost when the house burned. I remember this piece well," Aurore said, fingering the pendant. "This is the diamond pendant that Mr. Davco gave her when Serena was born. Eleanor loved it. She wore it nearly every day. She even wore it when she posed for the portrait."

As if on cue, everyone turned to look at the portrait hanging on the wall of the staircase.

Recovered from the betrayal, Aurore lashed out. "How did you get these?"

"I started finding jewelry and old coins a few years back," Sam admitted. "They must have been turned over by the tractor when the house was rebuilt."

"You mean, there's more?" Tammie asked.

Aurore eyed him suspiciously. "How come you never said anything?"

"What happened to the rest, Sam?" Dylan pressed.

Sam sighed and shook his head. "They're gone. I'm sorry, Aurore."

"What do you mean, gone? If you've found more of Mrs. Davco's jewelry, you need to give them back."

"I can't," Sam said. "You don't know how sorry I am."

"Let me guess," Dylan said. "You've got a friend down at the auction site who fenced them for you. It's been a sweet little deal for you all these years, so you haven't felt the need to say anything. What was it you said to me in the garden when I mentioned the state of the yard work? Oh, right—they're on a limited budget. Was this your way of getting a raise for yourself without anyone knowing?"

A small gasp escaped Aurore's lips. "Sam, how could you? And after Mr. Davco has been so good to you? I can't believe it. We kept you on after Mr. Davco went away. I should think you'd have been grateful."

"I didn't think anyone would mind a few pieces. Everyone thought they were gone, anyway. I didn't think anyone would miss them."

"That doesn't make it right," Tammie said.

Aurore straightened her back and pulled her robe tighter. "I won't press charges, Sam. That'd only upset Serena. And I won't tell her about this. It'd only break her heart. But I do expect you to get your things and leave this house this instant. We don't require your services any longer."

"I'm real sorry about this, Aurore. You have no idea."

"I am, too."

Sam left, and Aurore continued to look at the jewelry in her hand. "Serena will want these," she said.

Then she turned to Tammie. "Unless you thought they'd go to you…?"

Tammie's eyes widened, the hurt in them unmistakable. "You said that pendant was a gift when Serena was born. I think it's only right she get it, and the rest of the jewelry."

Aurore nodded and sighed. "Forgive me. It's no excuse, but I'm a little tired. And this is…upsetting."

"Apology accepted."

"I'll see to cleaning these pieces tomorrow morning. I suggest we turn in, and… Mr. Montgomery…what were you doing out there this late at night, anyway?"

"I was checking on Tammie."

Aurore nodded, and to Dylan's surprise, she didn't challenge him. "Good night."

She was halfway up the stairs when Aurore turned and said, "Make sure you lock your bedroom door."

"I will. Good night."

Tammie waited until Aurore was upstairs before she spoke to Dylan. "Do you believe Sam's story?"

Dylan made a face. "I don't know what to believe anymore."

Fatigue was pulling at him. Dark, puffy shadows were

under his eyes, and his shoulders had a slight droop, as if he could barely keep himself standing.

"You should go back to the campground and get some rest."

"I know, but…" He stared at her as if he wanted to say something but was holding back.

"I'll be fine here." She crossed her arms across her chest. "Now that I know there won't be any other strange men lurking outside tonight."

"Are you sure?"

"About what? Strange men, or that I'll be okay?"

He gave her a half smile that made him look completely…adorable. Why, she didn't know. He was wearing army fatigues and a black T-shirt that hung loosely around his frame. His hair was a mess, most probably from him rubbing his hand over his head to try to stay awake while he'd been outside. There was nothing Keanu Reeves-ish about Dylan Montgomery, and yet…

"I'm fine," she said.

But she wasn't. Sam Watson's midnight rounds in the garden had put her on edge. She wondered if he would come back tonight. What would keep him from digging up more valuables in the garden? It wasn't that she cared so much about him stealing. It was the creepy feeling that someone was always watching.

But she wouldn't tell Dylan that. Just because she was uncomfortable, that didn't mean Dylan should stay and risk falling asleep at the wheel because he'd stayed up all night watching the house. And she had a feeling he would, if she voiced her concerns.

She followed him to the door.

"Are you really okay?"

She answered honestly. "I don't know. I mean, it's just a scraped knee, but…"

"But what?"

She closed her eyes, felt his fingertips on her chin, lifting it ever so slightly. When she opened her eyes again, he was staring directly into her eyes.

"Tell me."

"After today, I'm not sure I'm strong enough to handle what I find out. That accident today—in part, it was my own fault."

His brow furrowed.

"No, really," she insisted. "I've been so preoccupied with finding out information about my parents. I kept thinking I had to talk to everyone, and I was so eager to talk to people that I wasn't paying attention. Maybe that man was right, and I just shouldn't have been there."

He nodded, but didn't appear convinced. "Do you really think that accident wasn't staged?"

"You think it was?"

He shrugged. "Did you see the name on the truck? Aztec Corporation?"

"What about it?"

"I've seen that name before, and I can't remember where. It's just a hunch, but it's worth checking out."

She lowered her head, feeling the weight of the day crashing around her. "No one knew we were going to be there," she said.

"But they knew we were in town. Being at the auction grounds was a logical next step. Hey, are you sure you're okay?"

She gave Dylan a weak smile. "I don't know if I'm strong enough to handle all this."

He looked at her, seemed to read the uncertainty she felt. Then he said, "You don't give yourself enough credit, lady. You're a lot stronger than you think."

"How can you tell?"

"Because the woman who came all the way across the country and made her way into this house after I tried for a month to do the same is incredibly smart...and brave. You may be feeling alone right now, Tammie, but you have to know this—not only is God with you, but I'm here, too."

Tears pressed against Tammie's eyes. Dylan had touched upon the exact sense of insecurity she'd been feeling. She'd struggled to stay strong, but everything she learned seemed to be pulling her farther away from her parents, instead of bringing her the closeness she sought.

"Thank you for that."

His voice was low when he spoke again. "You're welcome."

He bent his head and came closer to her. He was going to kiss her, she knew. Cupping her cheek, he pressed his lips tenderly to her mouth.

He wasn't in any hurry to break the connection, and neither was Tammie. She leaned into the kiss, reaching her arms up to his shoulders. Dylan's arm dropped to her waist. He linked his hands, enveloping her in his embrace in a way that made Tammie feel sheltered, not possessed.

She liked the feeling. She liked even better the way this man who was sometimes gruff, sometimes tender, was kissing her.

The kiss ended sooner than Tammie would have liked, leaving her dazed and unsteady on her feet.

Dylan's face registered shock, and he drew in a deep breath. "I'm s—"

"Don't. Don't say it," she said softly, placing her fingers gently against his lips. "I'm not."

His gaze lingered on her face as he placed his hand on her cheek again, rubbing it with the pad of his thumb. She leaned into the warmth of his touch, and her head began to swim. It felt good to be this close, to feel this connection to someone who understood. It had felt even better moments earlier, when she was in his arms.

Bending forward again, he kissed her head and said, "Good night, Tammie."

"Good night."

Tammie closed the door behind him, and Dylan stepped out onto the porch. The cool night air slapped him hard in the face as he stepped off the porch steps and onto the walkway.

Guilt crept into his mind. "The last thing she needed was a kiss from a guy she hardly knows, Dyl," he said to himself.

But as he walked up the path, he thought of how nice Tammie had felt in his arms, the feeling that had enveloped him and still hung on.

"This isn't what I came here for, Lord," he muttered, looking at the bright stars up in the sky as he walked the short distance to his Jeep with unsteady legs. "I didn't expect to feel this way about her."

When he got to the place where he'd parked his Jeep, he climbed in and gunned the engine. With the top off, it was going to be a cold ride back to the campground, but it would keep him awake and alert.

Tomorrow he'd go to the library and check to see if Sonny had e-mailed him the information he'd asked for. If she hadn't, it'd be time to call in favors from a few friends in Chicago. This small town's resources were limited. He needed a big-city computer and a few people who were good at sniffing out facts. Sonny was more than capable, but he needed someone with access she didn't have.

But all that could wait until tomorrow morning. He needed to shake off this feeling that had him reeling. For so many years, he'd been alone. Oh, he had a loving family with Sonny, Cash and their parents. He had more cousins than he knew the names of. He was rich with family.

Sonny hadn't had to push that hard to get him to leave the Marines, he realized. He'd been ready. All he'd really needed was a reason to go in another direction. He just wished he'd timed it better, come home before Cash had gotten into whatever trouble caused him to disappear.

Family had always been important to Dylan. But he'd never concentrated on having a family of his own. After that kiss with Tammie tonight, thoughts of what he'd been missing drifted in and out of his mind. But he needed her to help find Cash. He was sure of that. And he didn't need to have anything cloud his thinking.

And yet, as he pulled onto the road that led to the campground, he wondered if a little clouding might just do him good.

TEN

Tammie looked at her reflection in the mirror as she brushed her teeth in her private bathroom. She'd somehow managed to get showered, fully dressed, and put together, but she was still half asleep.

After Dylan left last night—or rather midmorning—sleep had been impossible, for a lot of reasons, not the least of which was the way Dylan had kissed her.

Serena had been quiet last night, but every once in a while, Tammie had heard sounds from the other side of the bedroom wall. Tammie had struggled to hear, but couldn't make out a word of what Serena was saying.

She'd go to her this morning and talk to her. She was determined to find out the truth about what was going on in this family. In this house.

"Will you be having breakfast this morning?" Susan asked as Tammie walked out the door into the hallway. Susan held a tray of food. She walked past Tammie and stopped at Serena's bedroom door.

Tammie wasn't hungry, but she decided it would get Susan out of Serena's room if she had to go back downstairs to fix breakfast for her.

"I'd love some scrambled eggs," she said, seeing how Serena's plate was filled. "And that orange juice looks good, too."

"Would you like some buttered toast?" Susan asked.

"No. Eggs will be enough. Thank you. I'll take this one in to Serena."

"But I was just going to feed her."

"I can take care of that while you get my eggs. Serena might like having someone eat with her, instead of just feeding her."

"She needs her strength. Make sure she drinks all her juice."

"I will. Thanks."

She took the tray from Susan's hands and went into the room. Aurore was already there, propping Serena up with pillows.

Lord, am I ever going to get a moment's peace?

She chose her words carefully. "Did she have a good night?"

Aurore didn't look up, just held Serena by the chin and looked into her eyes.

"She's awake enough to eat. I need to get some nourishment into her. My poor girl seems to be wasting away on me."

"I'll do it." Aurore looked up then, saw the tray Tammie was holding in her hands. "Is there a problem with that?"

Aurore shook her head slightly. "She may not take anything from you."

"If she doesn't, I'll call for help."

Aurore paused a moment. "I can understand why you think it is so important to be here."

"Do you? Do you really?" The tray was getting heavy

in Tammie's hands and the muscles in her arms were beginning to protest. She wanted to put the tray down, but she held it firm.

"Yes. But I don't think you'll find what you're looking for. Your parents died, Tammie. I know you're upset, but you can't get them back by digging up the past."

"Why did they take me from here?"

"I can't give you that answer."

"You can't—or won't?"

"Does it matter?"

"To me it does. You knew my mother. I know you did."

Aurore straightened. "Yes, your mother and I were very close friends."

Tammie hadn't expected Aurore's words, or her own reaction to them. She couldn't wrap her mind around any of this. How could Aurore have been her mother's *close* friend all these years and she not know it?

"You were?" she asked incredulously.

"Don't act so surprised. We both grew up here in Eastmeadow. We went to school together from the time we were in elementary school. By now you know your parents lived here, worked here."

At Tammie's shocked expression, Aurore added, "I assumed you knew. I thought… How did you end up here?"

Aurore walked across the length of the floor, grabbed the tray from Tammie's hand. "Let me take this before you drop it. Her eggs are getting cold."

"Who's Dutch?"

Aurore kept her gaze on Serena, who started to stir in the bed. "How do you know that name?"

"I found a letter with my mother's things. It mentioned

closing up their house and taking care of things. I didn't know my mother had lived here all her life. I just found the letter…"

Aurore offered up the first smile Tammie had seen from her. If you could really call it a smile. "And you were curious."

"That doesn't mean I've found what I'm looking for."

"And you won't. It doesn't exist. Not the way you want it to exist."

"What about Cash Montgomery? He existed."

The mention of Dylan's brother's name got a reaction from Aurore. "Don't bother trying to deny that Serena knows him. Dylan showed me the picture of the two of them. It's clear they had a relationship."

"What makes you think that?"

Tammie sighed. "Please. Don't insult me by pretending they didn't know each other."

"Oh, Serena knew Cash Montgomery. She met him when she was in college."

Tammie stopped short. After so many secrets, for Aurore to suddenly give up information freely was a little unsettling. Just when she thought she knew how to handle the woman, Aurore tossed her a curveball.

"That must have been about ten years ago or so."

"Actually, Serena didn't attend college until quite a few years after she'd been out of high school."

"Because of her illness?"

Aurore shook her head. "There were a lot of reasons. She never finished. College, that is. She couldn't handle the course load, because it caused too much stress."

"She looked fine in the picture I saw. She looked happy."

"Pictures are deceiving."

"Dylan never mentioned Cash being a college student just a few years ago," Tammie said. She was fishing for information. She had no idea that Cash had even gone to college, let alone when he would have gone.

Aurore glanced at her and smirked. "He wasn't a student."

"Oh."

Then Aurore bent over and kissed Serena on the head. "If you insist on feeding her, make sure she drinks. She needs it. I don't want her to become dehydrated." She moved the bedside cart with the food tray next to the bed. "She has a hard time feeding herself in this state, so you'll have to do all the work. And it could get messy."

She sighed and looked at Tammie, and her mouth moved as if she were going to say something more. But then she just walked to the door.

"Why won't you say it?"

With her hand on the doorknob, Aurore asked, "What?"

"That I'm Eleanor Davco's daughter. Why won't you just admit it?"

Aurore's eyes glassed over. "Connie always told me you were like Eleanor. She would be pleased. To this day, I still miss her. I miss both of them."

When she was gone, Tammie realized that was probably the closest Aurore would come to admitting she was Serena's sister.

Her eyes were blurry from unshed tears. Dylan had said she was strong, but she didn't know how much of the truth she could take. The truth about why her parents had taken her away and why they had never told her she had a sister.

Serena was staring at her. Her eyes were vacant, but

every once in a while Tammie saw some sign of recognition. Almost as if Serena were trying to break free.

"Are you hungry, Serena?" she asked, not knowing what else to say.

"B-Babies. They steal b-b-abies." Her voice was soft and weak.

Tammie lifted from the chair and put her face in front of Serena's. "You are in there, my sister. I know you are. I know you're trying to tell me something. I pray you'll be able to tell me everything soon."

But Serena's eyes went blank again, and Tammie felt the weight of defeat on her shoulders.

The door opened, and Susan came in with another tray of scrambled eggs. Even though Tammie had specifically said she didn't want buttered toast, Susan had gone to the trouble of making it.

"Thank you. I'll take it from here," Tammie said.

Susan left the room with a frosty glare.

"I'm going to take care of you, Serena. I promise you that. But you need to keep up your strength. You need to drink something."

She lifted the cup of orange juice to Serena's lips, but then she paused and pulled the cup away. Serena had changed since she'd come to the mansion. On the day Tammie arrived, Serena had been much more lucid. What had changed to make her this way?

What if it wasn't really mental illness that was keeping Serena bedridden? She certainly looked fine in the photo Dylan had given her. What if Aurore and Susan really didn't want Serena to talk to her and Dylan?

Tammie shook her head at her own thoughts. What

possible reason would they have for doing that to Serena? Despite everyone in the house being a little off, it did appear that they had genuine concern for her well-being.

"Oh, Tammie, girl," she muttered to herself. "You're starting to get a little too paranoid."

Serena shook her head slowly and blinked her eyes, as if she was forcing herself to do it. The movements were slight, but Tammie caught them and looked directly at her sister.

"If you can understand me, Serena, do that again."

Serena blinked and shook her head.

Smiling, Tammie looked at the food on Serena's tray, then at hers. Would they poison her, as well?

"I've got to be out of my mind," Tammie whispered, with what sounded to her like a slightly hysterical laugh. "Do you want to eat this, Serena?"

Serena shook her head weakly.

"Then don't," she said, dropping the fork on the plate and pushing the eggs away. "I'll come back with food for you. I'll make it myself."

If the food was laced with drugs, what would they put it in? The eggs? Probably not. The heat would probably weaken the effect of any drugs. The juice? Possibly. She wasn't going to take any chances on any of it.

She looked at the food Susan had brought in for her. The staff knew that Dylan was keeping a close watch over her while she was here. If anything happened to her, they had to know they wouldn't get away with it. But who was looking out for Serena?

"I won't let anything happen to you," she said, looking into her sister's vacant eyes.

"Serena? Do you hear me?" It was as if Serena were

looking right through her, not seeing her at all. Then her eyes shifted and her mouth moved, but Tammie couldn't make out what she was trying to say.

"Babies?" Tammie asked. "They're stealing babies? Whose babies?"

But then Serena was gone again, lost to whatever had a hold on her.

"You are in there. I know you are. And I'm going to help you, so you can finally tell me what you've been trying to say since I arrived."

Taking the drink and the plate of eggs to the private bathroom, she poured half of the eggs down the toilet and two thirds of the glass of juice. There was no use letting anyone think Serena had drunk the whole glass, if she didn't normally do so. Better to let them think she'd consumed some of it.

When she got back to the room, Serena's eyes were brighter and she was sitting rigid against the pillow, as if it were taking every ounce of energy she had.

"What is it, Serena?" Tammie touched her sister's cheek, felt the sweat that was bubbling on her skin.

"They're…stealing…babies…. They'll…take you away… too."

"She's worse," Tammie said, climbing into Dylan's Jeep. They'd gotten a late start, because Dylan had slept so late. He was kicking himself for not setting the alarm on his cell phone so that he could have gotten here earlier.

Tammie's face was drawn and marred with worry. He let the engine idle.

"How much worse can she get?" he asked.

"Aurore mentioned giving Serena sedatives. I think it's the drugs that are making her like this. I think they're giving her too much."

He was silent for a moment, thinking about the possibility. He could tell she was waiting for a response.

When he offered none, she said, "Okay, I know. You think I'm being paranoid. Yeah, I've already gone there myself. I'm way past you're-on-to-something to the point where I'm beginning to think I might just join Serena in that other world she's in."

"It's a pretty strong accusation. But given Serena's mental state so far, I wouldn't put it past Aurore or Susan to overmedicate her to keep her quiet."

Tammie nodded and stared at the trees by the old barn at the back of the mansion. He was anxious to get to the library to use the computer, but he wasn't going to rush Tammie.

"Serena repeated what she'd said the other night."

"About stealing babies?"

"Yes. But then she said, 'They'll take you away, too.'"

He rubbed his jaw. He hadn't had time to shave this morning, and his face was starting to itch. "Cryptic."

"Unsettling."

"I wonder who 'they' are?"

Tammie sighed. "I don't know. But Aurore…she finally admitted I'm Eleanor Davco's daughter."

Dylan turned to her. No wonder Tammie was having a hard morning. "Wow" was all he could think to say.

"Yeah, I know." She chuckled nervously. "I mean, it's not like the evidence wasn't overwhelming enough for me to know it on my own. But hearing her actually admit it took me a little by surprise."

He cleared his throat. "About last night…"

He hadn't intended to blurt it out, but he'd wondered all morning if she'd thought at all about the kiss they'd shared. It wasn't as if Tammie didn't have a million other things on her mind. Kissing him had to be dead last on her list of things to worry about.

He'd tried not to think about it on the drive over. But he'd finally decided it would be better to just get it out, so that there was nothing in the way of them getting down to business once they got to the library.

And yet…the more time he spent with Tammie, the more he realized there was a hole in his life that needed filling. And that kiss had done a pretty good job of starting that.

"You must be exhausted," she said. "You left the mansion very late." She was talking about fatigue, but the softness of her expression told Dylan she knew he hadn't been talking about his lack of sleep.

Okay. He got the point. Either she didn't want to relive it or she'd decided there were more important issues at hand. Whichever it was, the moment was gone.

Dylan pressed the clutch and then the gas pedal. "We should start at the library first."

"The library?"

"I need to use the computer, and it's probably a good idea to check some old newspaper clippings. There should be information there you can use to find out about the Davco family. Possibly even the fire. If it was big news, the way people seem to remember, the local paper should have something on it."

"That library is rather small."

"True. But even if the library hasn't been brought into the twenty-first century, they must have town history written down somewhere. Maybe even old newspapers on microfilm, which would make things easier to search. Anyway, it's a good place to start."

"I appreciate you helping me like this," Tammie said. "I mean, you're spending all this time helping me find out information about my parents, when you should be looking for Cash."

"Oh, but I am. Something tells me the whole thing is related and wrapped around Serena Davco—somehow. If I find the answer to one, maybe the dead-end I've been sitting at will turn into an open road to answers."

She bit her bottom lip. "Speaking of Cash, Aurore also admitted that Serena knew him."

He took his eyes off the road for a second. "What did you do? Put truth serum in her coffee?"

"Very funny. I don't know why she was so open, except that maybe she figures we're going to find out anyway, so why keep up the pretense?"

"Did you show her the picture?"

"No, but I mentioned it. She said they met while Serena was in college, a few years back."

He thought about it a moment. "The timing sounds about right."

"Did Cash go to college then?"

Dylan shook his head and shifted gears. "No, but he often worked on drug raids at colleges."

"I think Serena was talking about me, Dylan. I think Serena knows who took me when I was a baby, and she might have told Cash. That's why they didn't want you here and they've been so protective about people getting close to Serena."

"They're afraid someone is going to find out the truth."

Dylan drove for a while longer, silently looking at the road and nothing else. Tammie stared out the window as they passed a large farm. The farmer was on a tractor out in the fields, a large cloud of dust trailing behind him as he moved.

As she looked at the fields, Tammie thought of how different her life could have been. She would have grown up here. It was beautiful, but no more so than the small Oregon town that had been her home.

"Are you okay?" she asked, when she suddenly realized how tense Dylan had become.

He sighed, shook his head. "I haven't been okay about this in a long while."

"I'm sorry," she said, reaching across and placing her hand over his on the stick shift. She let it linger there. Dylan didn't seem in any hurry for her to move it. "This must be very hard on you."

"I was away too long," he said. "There's a whole lot about my brother that I didn't know, and that's upsetting. I feel like I failed him somehow."

"It takes two to create distance. He could have come to you with his problems."

"In his own way, he did. But for some reason, he didn't confide in me about everything. I can see even in that picture that he cared for Serena. She's not just some girl he met on a job."

He finally pulled his hand away, rubbing his hand over the shadow on his jaw. To her surprise, the separation jarred her. She'd meant to give him comfort, but she was startled to realize how much she'd liked the connection.

"I don't know. I guess I always thought if there was a special woman in his life, he would have told me, you know?"

He paused, downshifted and took the left turn onto Main Street. Tammie held on to her seat as he made the turn. Then he hit the gas and accelerated again.

"Let's just get to the library. I need to check some things out."

The old stone-faced building was in the middle of town, across the street from the white church on the hill. Both buildings looked almost lost amid the throng of cars, vans and trucks parked on every available inch of grass. People stood at the entrance to the church parking lot, waving orange flags to get motorists' attention and convince them to pay money to park on the church grounds. A quick glance up Main Street and there were more people with orange flags herding cars deep into the fields.

It was difficult to get around, now that the auction was in full swing. Unlike yesterday, when they'd been able to drive into town and park, they had to sit in bumper-to-bumper traffic before finding room in one of the makeshift parking lots.

They backtracked to the library, walking past people with empty carts that they'd obviously hoped to fill with a deal or two at the antique auctions.

Dylan held the library door open. As she walked inside, Tammie took a moment to let her eyes adjust to the light. The air inside was stuffy, as if the air-conditioning hadn't yet been turned on and the windows weren't providing sufficient air circulation.

Tammie breathed in deeply and followed Dylan up to a small table where a woman was sitting and checking in a pile of books. While he was talking to the woman, she took a moment to look around the room. The library was small in comparison to any library she'd ever seen, although it seemed to make the most of every inch of space. Stacks of books were everywhere, and the shelves had little room for two people to pass through. She imagined there probably wasn't a lot of money to keep the library going and doubted it would hold any information of real value to them.

In the far corner, by a set of open windows, sat a table with three computers. Beyond that, toward the back of the building, was a doorway to another room.

"They have an Internet connection here. I'm going to check my e-mail first. We lucked out. All the local newspapers are on microfiche, all the way back to the fifties."

She tilted an eyebrow. "Lucky? That'll take forever to look through."

"What did you expect?" he said, keeping his voice low. "Twenty-first-century technology? I'd say we're lucky to have this much. It's a lot better than sifting through dusty, old crumbling newspapers in a vault."

"You have a point."

The woman behind the table stamped the last book and added it to the pile. Then she got up and walked over to them.

"This is Mrs. Martinez," Dylan said, introducing Tammie to the woman. "Mrs. Martinez, this is Tammie Gardner. She came all the way out here from Oregon."

Mrs. Martinez's gaze lingered on Tammie's face for a brief moment. "Amazing. Lois Caulfield said the resemblance was striking, but I said it couldn't be that close a resemblance."

"Mrs. Caulfield?" Dylan said.

"She's a schoolteacher in town, but she works a tent down at the auctions as a second job. She was Serena Davco's teacher early on, and tutored her some at home when she was under the weather. She saw that load of furniture tumble from the truck and nearly hit you. At first she thought it was Serena, until someone told her your name."

"She knew Serena well, then?"

Mrs. Martinez started toward the back room. "We all know Serena. She was such a sweet girl growing up. I'll just get that microfiche from the vault and set you up."

Dylan made a comical face when Mrs. Martinez turned her back. "They really do have a vault," he said quietly.

Mrs. Martinez apparently heard. "Oh, yes. This used to be the town hall years ago, but the town grew too big. They used to have town meetings right there in the church across the street."

"How interesting," Tammie said.

Dylan stopped at the table with the computers. "I'll meet you out back," he said, sitting down at the computer closest to the room Mrs. Martinez had disappeared into.

"Now you're looking for information about the fire, the young man said?"

"Yes, and any newspaper articles from the weeks after that."

"I remember the fire, but I was quite young at the time. I don't recall the month." Mrs. Martinez handed Tammie a box. "Here are the boxes for that year. I'm afraid you'll have to look through them to find the dates you're looking for. We try to keep them in order, but people don't always put them back in the right place."

Tammie took the disks and after a moment's hesitation, asked, "Someone mentioned something about a scandal with the church around the time of the fire. Do you remember that?"

Mrs. Martinez thought a minute. "Scandal? Not that I recall. My family moved to Eastmeadow around that time, but I can't say I remember ever hearing about a scandal with Pastor Robbins. He's the only pastor I've known." She took Tammie's hand and gave it a gentle squeeze. "If you need me, I'll be right out front. This should get you started, though."

Tammie settled in the back room, at the microfiche machine. The disks were labeled with the year, but not the month.

"I have a feeling it's going to be a long afternoon," she muttered.

From where she was sitting, she could see Dylan settled into a chair at the computer closest to the doorway. He was quite a handsome man, strong and resolute. That kind of strength wasn't just in muscle, but in character. That much was already evident to her, even after the short time she'd known him.

As she absentmindedly looked at the dates on the black and white films whizzing past on the screen, she thought of what it had felt like last night, when Dylan kissed her. There had been many times she imagined herself with a man, sharing her life, her faith. For months after her parents' deaths, she hadn't thought of dating at all. She no longer pictured the life ahead of her the way little girls dreamed. It was if she'd been stuck in a quagmire for far too long. The thought of walking down the aisle without her father's arm hooked around hers…well, it all seemed so painful.

Something about Dylan brought those thoughts of family and the future back to her mind. But she quickly pushed them aside as she glanced at the dates on the fiche.

"February," she muttered to herself. She'd been born in June and Mr. Beaumont had told her he'd been working at the auction grounds the night of the fire and remembered the glow. It made sense to check the month of June for any news about the auction and then go from there.

She changed the film and began searching again. Every so often, Tammie would glance over at Dylan. He was sitting in a chair that seemed almost too small for his frame. He was reading details on the monitor intently, and every so often, he typed fast, his face drawn into an adorable frown.

Adorable?

"Oh, puh-leeze, Tammie…" she whispered to herself, rolling her eyes.

She had no time for this. There was more at stake than the way she'd felt when Dylan Montgomery kissed her or when he held her last night. She needed to remember that.

Her mind was only half taking in the information on the microfiche until she came upon a small article announcing the upcoming auction. A picture of Main Street and the white church across the street was splashed on the page, as well. It looked much as it did today, with hordes of people roaming the streets. The only difference was that it looked like it was in a time warp, with fancy old cars that today would be considered collectors' items.

As she slowly moved her fingers, changing from frame

to frame, her mind was at war. She needed to concentrate on the fire at the mansion and any mention of Eleanor or Byron Davco.

"How's it going?"

Tammie hadn't even heard Dylan come up behind her, but the sound of the chair being dragged across the floor made her jump. He sat down next to her and glanced over her shoulder. She could feel the heat from his body as he sat down next to her, smell the clean scent of soap and something more enticing. She closed her eyes for a brief moment, then focused on the screen again.

"I'm just coming up on the month I was born."

"Good. We should start to see something, then. When's your birthday?"

"June fourteenth."

"Assuming that's your real birthday, let's check there."

It had never occurred to Tammie that the day she knew as her birthday could be wrong. Suddenly, that one small detail seemed vitally important. She didn't want that taken away from her when so much else had been already.

The day she knew as her birthday came around. "Nothing," Tammie said. "Just mentions of the auctions and a livestock fair in another town."

Dylan moved his hand over the microfiche knob, covering her hand with his. Without thinking, she turned her hand over until her fingers locked with his. Dylan looked away from the screen and at her face. So many things were running through her mind, her head began to swim. She blinked to steady herself and pulled her hand away.

When she found her voice, she said, "Move ahead one day."

It took a moment for him to turn his attention to the screen and move the frame forward. When he did, Tammie drew in a slow breath.

Then the newsprint practically exploded with detail.

"Bull's-eye," she said as mixed feelings collided. On the one hand, she wanted to find out the truth. But how much did she really want to see?

The front page headlines screamed that Eleanor Davco, daughter of one of the town's oldest families, had been killed in a tragic fire. Tammie's hand went to her chest, and she forced herself to breathe. There was a picture of Eleanor Davco. She couldn't have been much older than Tammie was now.

Dylan read ahead. "The house wasn't completely destroyed, but the damage was extensive. If your mother had just given birth to you, that may have been the reason she wasn't able to escape the fire."

"My birth mother," Tammie said quietly. With each word she read, she felt as if the woman who had raised her, the parents she still mourned, were being ripped from her arms. She couldn't quite bring herself to say that Eleanor Davco was her mother, even though she knew she was the woman who'd given birth to her.

Dylan glanced at her, seemed to sense her unease. But without saying a word, he put a gentle hand on her back to comfort her. Tammie wanted to curl into that comfort, but she kept to her task.

"There's no mention of a baby. At least not what I can see," Dylan said. He reached over and advanced the page forward again.

Tammie couldn't move. It was as if she were frozen in

place, trying to take in all the details. She didn't know what she'd have done if she'd had to look through all this alone.

"Wait," she said, putting her hand on his arm, when something caught her eye. "Backtrack a bit."

"What is it?"

"I don't know."

She put her hand on the microfiche control and slowly scrolled until she found what had caught her eye. It hadn't been front-page news, like the Davco mansion fire, but it had been news.

"That's my father's picture," she said, tears springing to her eyes. "I don't remember him being that young."

"You were an infant when this was taken."

"The money went missing the night of the fire," she said, the shock of reading about her parents paralyzing her.

When she didn't read on, Dylan continued. "'Pastor Gardner and his wife have not been available for questioning regarding the missing funds. Town officials are urging the state police to inquire about the missing pastor and his wife and the allegations that they—'"

"Pastor? My father was a pastor? This is saying they stole money from the church. I don't believe it," she said as she speed read through the article. Tears blurred her vision, and her bottom lip wobbled. Unable to see anymore, she sat back in the seat and let Dylan read on. "This was the scandal Mr. Beaumont was talking about. My parents were part of this scandal. Does it say when they left?"

"This article just says that they hadn't been found for questioning. Let's look ahead."

He hesitated, and she felt his body stiffen next to her.

Tammie could barely feel her hands moving on the microfiche controls. Through her tear-filled eyes, she fought to see the newsprint on the screen.

"Here," Dylan said, stilling her hand and backing up.

While the first article was on page three, this article was buried on page nineteen.

"This one says more of the same. Pastor Gardner and his wife are still being sought for questioning regarding the missing funds. They were last seen—" Tammie stopped short.

"That's the night of the fire," Dylan added.

Tears were rolling down her cheeks. *Oh, Lord, what happened?* "I've got to get out of here," she said, pulling herself away from the microfiche machine and standing up, unable to take in any more.

ELEVEN

Tammie spun around to look at Dylan. His face was sympathetic, and his eyes filled with a warmth that was hard for her to look at. She couldn't. She didn't want sympathy or reason or understanding. She just wanted someone to tell her that all these lies about the two people she'd loved most in the world weren't true.

"I have to get out of here."

She ran through the library and pushed out the door right into the busy street.

Without looking where she was going, she stepped off the curb and almost walked into traffic before a local cop pulled her back by the arm.

"Hold on a second, young lady. The antiques will still be there when the traffic goes by."

Tammie was only marginally aware that the cop had stopped traffic for her and was motioning her to cross. Her feet and legs moved with a will of their own. Stunned was the only way she could have described herself.

All this time, she'd been searching for something. She'd wanted the truth, wanted to confirm her suspicions that her parents' deaths hadn't been some random accident.

Someone had to be responsible for this. And yet she hadn't expected this.

Had someone killed them because they were criminals? Stealing church funds, and then—?

She didn't want to think about any of it. She ran up the hill, around the cars lining the church grounds, past the people waving orange flags, and she kept moving until she reached the church doors. All the while, she never looked back.

Dylan raced after Tammie. She'd looked as if she were ready to pass out. But when he walked out the library doors into the crowd, he'd lost her for a brief moment, until he saw her running through the parked cars and up the church steps.

He kept running until he reached the church, then took the granite steps two at a time. He yanked the door open and stepped inside, pausing only long enough for his eyes to adjust to the change in light.

Dylan had always believed that God was everywhere. If he was on an op in the middle of a war-torn area of the world, he'd felt God's presence surrounding him. Even when he saw the worst war had to offer, he'd relied on his faith that the Lord had a purpose, even where no man wanted to go.

When he was away from home, he always missed the sense of rightness he felt when he walked into church. There was something about walking into the Lord's home that always gave him a sense of peace. He felt it now, even though his turmoil continued to churn deep inside.

Tammie was sitting in a pew in the center of the church. Her light sobs echoed off the walls and tore at his heart.

Not wanting to disturb her, he slipped into a seat, but kept his distance, close to the end of the aisle.

"I should have told you," he said quietly, regret eating at him. "Even if I didn't know for sure, I should have prepared you for it."

Her face was wet with tears when she looked at him. "You knew about all this?"

"That your father was a pastor here in this church, and that there was a question that money was taken? Yes, I found that out yesterday. But I didn't want to tell you until I knew it was more than just rumor. That was wrong of me."

"I don't know what I expected," she said quietly, her head bowed as if she were in prayer. "I'd prayed so often these last few weeks that I'd find the truth. But now…"

"Maybe you should ask God for comfort in finding the truth, and for understanding why they made the decision not to tell you. I know it must be hard for you."

"Hard doesn't quite cover it." Tammie rubbed her eyes. "I didn't know them at all, Dylan," she said, looking at him with an expression that told him she'd given up.

He hated to think she'd been brought to that. Even when there was no hope, there was something that kept you moving forward. Any fight Tammie had had in her before was gone now, and it shattered something inside Dylan to see it.

"You've come this far, Tammie. There's still more to learn."

She laughed—sounded almost like a small sob—and shook her head. "I'm not sure I want to know more. Maybe Bill was right. No good can come from me finding out the truth. I should have listened to him and never come here."

"Bill?"

"A friend. He didn't want me to come. Maybe he was right."

Jealousy suddenly kicked Dylan in the gut. He didn't want to ponder who this Bill guy was to Tammie. She'd never mentioned a boyfriend, and he'd have thought she would have by now.

"You don't mean that," he said, reaching across the back of the pew and placing his hand on her shoulder. He gave it a gentle squeeze, but pulled it away when she tensed.

"Are you sure? I keep trying to figure out if there is some possible reason why I ended up with them instead of Byron Davco. If I survived the fire and Eleanor didn't, then someone had to know. As much as I don't want to believe it, I think they stole me, just like the church funds, Dylan. If it were any other reason, they would have said something. They would have told me I was adopted. But if they were…criminals…"

"You don't really believe that, do you?"

"How can I not? The people of this town believed my parents, Aaron and Connie Gardner, were criminals, that they stole that money. Did they know about me, too? Did anyone even ask about me?"

"There was no mention of a baby in any of the articles we read. Just an investigation of the church funds."

She swayed in her seat.

Dylan couldn't stand it anymore. She was shattered, and there wasn't a thing he could do to make it better for her. He moved closer and drew her into his arms. She didn't fight him. Instead, she sank against his chest and sobbed with her hands covering her face.

"They lied to me. My whole life, they lied to me." She

looked up and took a deep breath. "And I think that's what I'm having the hardest time with. I can't…forgive them for it. I know I should, and I've tried. But every time I learn something new about my life, it's so awful. I'm just so…angry with them, and I can't tell them that. I can't look my mother and father in the face and tell them how angry I am or ask them why!"

"If you felt any different, I'd question it," he said. "You have a right to feel hurt and betrayed about something so important. Don't forget that, or be too hard on yourself because you can't let it go."

She closed her eyes, trying to compose herself, and he waited. He'd wait all afternoon if he had to. He was struck forcefully by how right Tammie felt in his arms, as if this was where she was meant to be. It should have scared him. He'd never felt this way about a woman before, and certainly not after such a short time. But he couldn't deny this attraction, or the way it moved him.

"Do you think Cash knew? Do you think that's why he's missing?"

"Let's not get ahead of ourselves. Don't forget, Cash has only been missing for a few months. Your parents have been gone almost two years."

"But you said you thought the two were somehow connected."

"Yes, in some way. But if the evidence doesn't point in that direction, I can't allow myself to get muddled by what-ifs."

Tammie sniffed. "Then what? What could he possibly have found out from Serena? And what about the drug charges?"

"Cash worked for the DEA, which is why it was so

easy for the authorities to believe the charges against him. It happens—good cop turns bad. In his case, good agent gets caught with the goods. But it didn't go down that way. He was framed. I just need to find out by whom."

"If someone was really framing him for something, and it had to do with Serena, it had to be more than him finding out that Eleanor Davco's baby had survived the fire. I mean, after all this time, why would it matter? Who besides Byron Davco even cared? Eleanor's not alive. Byron Davco is in a nursing home and doesn't even remember his family. Who'd have something to gain from this that possibly had that kind of power to frame Cash?"

Dylan swallowed. "Aztec Corporation."

"Who?"

"Did you see the name of the company selling those statues yesterday?"

She shook her head and swiped her face of wetness.

"The reproductions that were smashed when the armoire went over. The name on the truck?"

"Oh, okay. I remember."

"It kept nagging at me. I'd seen the emblem on the truck before. I'd heard the name, but couldn't place it. Then I remembered something I'd seen at Cash's apartment after he'd gone missing."

"What was it?"

"It was just a package with a few scraps of paper tucked away. I'd gone looking for pictures, and when I found it I didn't pay it any mind. After I saw that statue at the Davco mansion, it triggered my memory, and I called my sister last night. Sonny is good at digging up information."

"Did she find out anything?"

"Not much on Aztec Corporation other than that they sell fake Aztec statues that aren't even remotely correct. Sonny was appalled." Dylan shrugged, knowing that if he'd been there, his sister would have gone on all night about it. "But this morning she e-mailed me about some postcards clipped together with the info on Aztec."

"What was it?"

"They were pictures of a shipment of paintings that were stolen some years back. One of them surfaced on the black market about six months ago and opened an investigation."

"What does this have to do with anything?"

"The paintings were stolen about two months before you were born."

"Do you think it's related?"

He cocked his head to one side and thought a moment. "Maybe. I can't say for sure. It could be a coincidence."

With one eyebrow raised, she said, "There are no coincidences."

He smiled at that. "That sounds like something I'd say. Why Cash would have either of those things hidden in a drawer, I can't say. But I don't want to jump the gun. It's worth checking Aztec Corporation out a bit more. Sonny said it's quite a large company, though, and it may be hard to find anything useful."

"What about the stolen piece that resurfaced?"

The church was quiet except for their voices. But the window was open, and every so often the sound of a blaring horn from a car stuck in traffic cut into the quiet.

"I have a friend in Chicago who is pulling some strings to get a copy of the police report. But all that is low priority."

"Valuable paintings being discovered is low priority?"

"The original owner is dead, and the painting was returned to the estate. The police aren't looking for the thieves, because they can't prosecute. The statute of limitations is up. From what Sonny uncovered, there isn't any information about where the paintings came from or where they've been. It simply said *private collection*."

"Strange."

He hadn't been in any hurry to let go of Tammie. He liked a whole lot how it felt, just sitting there holding her. But the realness of just how dangerous a world Cash had stepped into was becoming startlingly apparent.

He took her hand and squeezed it. "Pray with me?"

His words washed over Tammie, and something shifted inside her. She felt as if she were being led to water after days of roasting in the hot sun. Had she really distanced herself from the Lord so much since her parents' deaths that his simply taking her hand in prayer could move her so deeply?

In the silence, they prayed. Dylan whispered a prayer for Cash, and for the strength to see this journey through until he found him. And then for Tammie's parents, so that she could find peace with whatever truths she found.

It was only when she opened her eyes and wiped the tears that had filled them that Tammie saw the pastor standing in the doorway, staring at them.

TWELVE

The pastor lifted his hand. "Please, don't let me interrupt."

They returned to their position on the bench as the pastor slowly walked over to them.

"I don't often see people in prayer inside the church during auction week. It's nice to see some friendly faces."

"You must be Pastor Robbins," Dylan said.

"That I am," he answered with a smile.

The pastor looked at Tammie, took in her red-rimmed eyes. "What's troubling you, Serena? Has your father taken a turn for the worse?"

His face was sympathetic, and Tammie could feel tears surging to the surface again at his kindness. She was infinitely glad Dylan spoke.

"Pastor, this isn't Serena. Her name is Tammie. She's not from Eastmeadow."

His eyes widened. "I didn't realize Serena had any other relatives."

"We believe Tammie is Serena's sister."

He nodded. "The resemblance is uncanny. You could almost be twins."

Tammie flipped a lock of hair behind her ear. "Did you know the pastor that was here prior to you?"

"Just briefly. I was only here a short time before the Gardners left."

"Then you know about the scandal regarding the church funds?" Tammie blurted out.

He looked thoughtful. "Why all these questions about the prior pastor?"

"They were my parents," Tammie said quietly. "They raised me."

Pastor Robbins sat down in the pew in front of them. "Oh, I see."

"I don't think you do," Dylan said. "The Gardners left Eastmeadow the night of the Davco mansion fire, right?"

"These are probably questions better asked of them, not me. It was a very long time ago."

"Twenty-seven years," Tammie said. "But I can't ask them. They died nearly two years ago."

He drew in a deep breath and sighed. "I'm sorry to hear that. I knew them as good people. I always wondered if it was the money scandal that made them leave."

"Then you do remember it?"

"Yes, I was part of it."

Tammie sat up straighter, her attention fully on the pastor now. "You were?"

"Of course. Many of the townspeople were involved, as well. We'd been trying to raise money for a new youth program for poor children. Eleanor Davco and the pastor's wife—Connie, I believe her name was—were very active in it. From what I understand, they'd been very close friends since childhood. We'd managed to raise quite a sum of money. It surprised us all how generous people had been. But then it mysteriously disappeared."

"No one knows what happened to it?" Tammie asked.

"No. It never turned up. But you know how these things work. This is a small town. People were very upset."

"What happened?" Dylan asked.

"It did what all scandals do. It blew way out of proportion. Suddenly we weren't just talking about a few thousand dollars. The church books were suspect. The pastor was accused of stealing money from the church. Many of the church members called for an investigation."

"Hence, the scandal," Dylan said.

Pastor Robbins shrugged. "Right. Of course, the books were audited, and in the end they were found to be in perfect order. There was no money missing, except for the money that was raised for the youth group. The final investigation listed the charity money as probably being lost in the Davco mansion fire that night."

Tammie rubbed her eyes, which were stinging from her tears. "The papers never said anything about that."

"Unfortunately, scandalous news gets better headlines. And the fire was front-page news for weeks. It was awful. Of course, you must know about all that."

Dylan nodded. "Do you remember what happened that night?"

The pastor rubbed his chin. "I don't recall the cause of the fire. Because Pastor Gardner had already left, I gave the services for Mrs. Davco and the unborn baby."

Tammie's head shot up. "You gave services for the baby?"

"Yes, at Mr. Davco's request. He was quite devastated by their deaths, as you can imagine."

Dylan placed his hand over Tammie's. "Yes, I'm sure he was."

"Pastor, I believe that baby was me."

The pastor's eyes widened with shock, and he looked at both of them. He cleared his throat. "Well, that *is* a surprise."

Tammie had no doubt her biological father mourned both the loss of his wife and baby, but she couldn't help but wonder if he'd known she'd survived the fire. Someone had to have known.

"Are you folks staying in town?" the pastor asked.

"I'm staying with my sister."

He nodded knowingly and smiled. "I'm happy to hear that. Serena could use some family around her right now."

"Why do you say that?" Dylan asked.

"She's been very troubled this last year. She didn't begin coming to church services until about two or three years ago. I didn't really know her while she was growing up. Byron Davco had a lot of anger after his wife's death and separated from his faith. Eleanor Davco was a good Christian woman, very active in the church and I remember her bringing Serena here as a little girl."

He looked around the empty church and then added, "I always thought Byron would one day bring Serena back. Eleanor would have liked that. But God seemed to have reached her through that young man she'd met."

Dylan leaned forward and asked, "What young man?"

"I don't know his name. But they seemed quite in love. I never saw them around town, but they would come to services together on occasion. Not very often. I don't think he lived here in town. And I don't think I'd ever seen her as happy as she was when she was with him." The pastor laughed and added, "I'm not foolish enough to think it was just my sermons that made her smile."

Tammie smiled, as well. Serena had been in love with Cash. Somehow it made her feel good to know that all the sadness and pain Serena had experienced in her life was at least balanced by love.

If nothing else, Tammie had been gifted with love from her parents, had known the love of a mother for at least twenty-five years. Even if Connie Gardner hadn't been her biological mother, she'd shared that bond. Serena had been robbed of that.

Dylan pulled a picture of Cash out of his pocket and showed it to the pastor.

Pastor Robbins's eyes lit up with recognition. "Yes, that's the young man."

"Have you seen him recently?"

"Not in quite a few months. Nor have I seen Serena. But maybe now that you're staying with her, you can persuade her to come out to Sunday services. With the two of you, of course."

"Thank you, Pastor. I'd like that," Dylan said. "We'll see what we can do about getting Serena here. She's not feeling very well right now."

The pastor nodded.

"Maybe you could take a trip out to the Davco home for a visit," Tammie added. "I'm sure Serena would like that."

"Thank you for the invitation. I'll do that. I have some work to do in the office now. If you need anything else, even some counsel," he said, speaking directly to Tammie, "be sure to stop in. I always make time."

"Thank you. I'll remember that."

As Pastor Robbins walked away, Tammie turned to Dylan and gently placed her hand on his arm. Words were jumbled up in her brain, and she couldn't think of any that could adequately express what she was feeling. He seemed to understand, and told her so with a quick smile and the light brush of his hand across her back.

Then, wordlessly, he led her out of the church.

The warm early summer air felt good on her face as she stepped into the sunshine. It seemed her parents hadn't been criminals. The relief she felt was overwhelming.

And her mother had been Eleanor's best friend. Maybe there was a good reason why she'd ended up with her parents instead of Byron Davco. She just needed to find out what it was.

As they walked down the steps of the church, Tammie asked, "Do you think it was coincidence?"

"That they left the same night as the fire? The same night you were born? No," Dylan said resolutely. "And you don't, either. But just like the rumor of the church funds being stolen, there is an explanation to this, Tammie. You just have to have faith."

She stopped midway on the steps.

"What is it?" he asked, a look of concern marring his face.

Her smile was wider than it had been in weeks. She could feel it. "It's just…. You always do that."

His brow furrowed. "What?"

"Make me feel like everything is going to turn out right. It's been so long since I felt like I had…"

What could she say? She wasn't completely sure what she was feeling, except that the more time she spent with Dylan, the more she wanted to be with him.

Reaching out, he took her hand and tangled her fingers with his. "Just say it," he urged, coming up to the same step she was standing on. He towered over her, and yet she never felt overwhelmed by him.

"For the first time since my parents died, I feel like I'm not alone. I have you to thank for that."

Then he looked deeply into her eyes. Bending his head, he came closer to her. She knew he intended to kiss her, and that was just fine. She met him halfway.

His lips brushed against hers, gentle at first, but then with more meaning. Tammie reached her arms up to his shoulders, pulling him closer to her.

Her hands trembling on his shoulders, she pulled away from him and looked into his face. He appeared just as shaken as she felt by their kiss.

He didn't let her go. Instead, he wrapped his arms around her, gave her a warm embrace that felt like a promise, and didn't let her go.

She felt his warm breath on her head as he spoke. "Are you sure you want to go here, Tammie?"

"Does it scare you?"

"No," he said quickly. "I can't deny that my feelings for you have taken me by surprise. But I'm not sorry about them. I just want you to be sure about what you're feeling. There's so much going on right now, I don't want to get into something with you only to find out I've misread what's been going on between us."

Tammie pulled away and looked right into his eyes. "I'm not sure about a lot of things, Dylan. But one thing I'm absolutely sure of is the way I feel about you. I haven't felt more sure about anything in a long time."

* * *

He'd kissed her.

Again.

After the kiss they shared that night in the foyer, Dylan had convinced himself that it'd been a fluke. It was just two people running on anxiety and fear.

He'd felt like a heel the next morning when he woke up. The first thing he'd thought about was the way she seemed to fit so nicely in his embrace, like it was meant to be that way.

And then he'd kissed her again at the church. The way she looked at him, the way she felt in his arms, had let him know he wasn't alone in his feelings. Since then, the connection between the two of them had grown too strong to ignore.

Great timing, Dylan. The absolute last thing either of them needed right now was to get involved in a relationship, and yet…

He parked his Jeep against the curb in front of the Davco mansion, behind a flatbed truck.

"I wonder who this is," Tammie said, climbing out of the Jeep and staring at the truck.

Dylan recognized it as Trudie Burdett's. The flatbed was empty. All the furniture Dylan had seen Trudie with that day when he helped her by the side of the road would be down at the auction grounds now.

"We'll find out soon enough," Dylan said.

"Leave me alone!"

Dylan heard the screaming coming from the kitchen as soon as they walked through the door. It sounded as if pots and pans were being thrown and dishes were breaking. He and Tammie ran to the back of the house, where the sound of chaos grew louder.

Dylan put a protective hand in front of Tammie and pushed through the swinging kitchen door first.

"What's going on here?" he asked.

Serena was in her nightgown, running in circles around the workspace island in the center of the kitchen, Susan close behind her. Her face filled with relief when she saw Tammie.

"Tammie, don't let them do it! I don't want to sleep anymore! Don't let them do it!" she cried.

Tammie still stood behind him in the doorway. She started to advance into the kitchen fully, but he held her back with his hand.

"There's glass all over the place," he said. "Serena, stay still."

Along with the glass and broken dishes on the floor was spilled food and drink, as well as a rattan tray turned over and pushed aside.

"What have you done to her?" Tammie asked Susan accusingly, her voice near hysterics.

The woman glared at her indignantly. "She needs her medication. That's all. She's very upset."

"She has a right to be upset," Tammie snapped. "It's clear you've been drugging her through her food. I stopped giving it to her yesterday, and look at her now."

"You stopped giving her the medicine? How dare you interfere?" Susan yelled.

"She may have interfered," Dylan said, making a clear path by pushing the glass and debris aside with his foot, "but Serena's a lot better off like this, than half out of her mind with drugs."

"You think this is better?" Susan said, motioning with her hands to indicate Serena's wild state.

"At least she can speak for herself," Tammie said. "At least she's not comatose—the way you've been keeping her."

Susan shook her head angrily. "You have no right to interfere with her treatment."

"I have every right. I'm her sister, and I won't have you harming her."

"Aurore will not be happy about this."

Susan tried to hold Serena back by the arm, but Serena wrenched free and ran to Tammie. Dylan let her by, and she wrapped her arms around Tammie and began to cry uncontrollably.

"Take her in the other room, Tammie," Dylan said quietly. "Make sure she's all right."

Tammie left the room with Serena.

Serena had somehow managed to bypass the broken glass by going around the island, but he knew she should still be checked for cuts.

He followed them into the living room. Aurore and Trudie Burdett came in from the backyard through the French doors at the back of the living room.

"What's going on?" Aurore said, her expression one of panic.

"I was just wondering the same thing," Dylan said.

"It was an accident, Aurore," Susan said. "She wouldn't eat her food. She's gone wild again."

"The way you're drugging her, I'd say she has a right."

"I have never hurt Serena," Aurore said.

Trudie put her hand over her mouth, as if to stifle a sob. "It's too much. It's gone on too long, Aurore. We need to tell them."

"No," Aurore said, panic returning to her face. "Serena will be all right. I'll calm her down."

"No!" Serena cried, burying her head against Tammie.

Tammie looked as if she were about to burst into tears herself. "What have you done to her?"

"Why don't you just leave?" Susan said. "You're not welcome here."

"Susan," Aurore said quietly, placing a gentle hand on the maid's back.

Aurore's face seemed almost as disturbed as Serena's. "There's blood on the carpet. Check Serena's feet to make sure she didn't hurt herself. She doesn't always feel the pain of being cut."

It was then that Dylan noticed that Susan held a first aid kit in her hand.

Trudie grabbed the first aid kit. "Let me do it. She won't let you come within ten yards of her," she said, and sat down next to Serena, who continued to sob.

"I can't let this go on any longer, Aurore," Trudie said, lifting Serena's foot to inspect it. "Eleanor wouldn't have wanted this. We need help."

Aurore straightened her spine, as if she were trying to stay in control. She spoke deliberately. "It's gotten too far beyond that, and you know it."

Trudie threw her hands up in frustration. "We need help, Aurore! Don't you see that?"

"We can handle this. We just have to stay calm."

"Handle what?" Dylan asked.

"Nothing," Susan said. "It's private family business."

"Anything that has to do with Serena is my business," Tammie said, making Serena lean toward her so that Trudie could inspect the wound on her foot.

"They tried to kill her," Trudie said as she worked on Serena's foot. She looked at Dylan. "You saw it. You were there. That load of furniture falling was no accident."

She turned to Aurore, as if trying to drive her point home, and shook her head. "Aaron and Connie are dead and now Turgis's people have nearly succeeded in killing Tammie, for the love of God. Why won't you let this stop?"

"What do you know about my parents?" Tammie asked Trudie.

"Trudie, don't!" Aurore cried. "The poor girl has already been through so much."

"She has to know!"

"You don't know what you're doing, either of you," Susan said. "They'll come after all of us."

"Go clean the kitchen," Aurore said. "Please just go do as I ask."

Susan huffed off. "It's only going to get worse," she said as she pushed the swinging door to the kitchen with force. "It'll get worse! They'll come after us!"

It was what Dylan had suspected, but hearing Trudie confirm his suspicions had only made it all the more real. The image of Tammie splayed on the ground invaded his mind again. He recalled the way the armoire had splintered under its own weight. It would have killed her, had she not been so quick. The thought of that was enough to drive him mad.

He looked hard at the women. "Tell me more," he commanded.

"That rope was cut," Trudie said to Dylan. "After I lost furniture the other day, I had Maynard get me some thick rope at Handies Feed Store. My rope had been frayed, but the rope holding that armoire was thick enough to hold up that load, and the truck along with it. There was no way it could have been frayed. After you left, I checked. The rope had been sliced clean, and that armoire was perched on the end of the truck on purpose. The only one who'd do that was someone who intended for that rope to break."

Aurore's face was ashen as Trudie turned to her.

"Don't you see? They tried to get to Tammie. They nearly killed her, Dutchie. You know Eleanor would never have wanted her baby girl put in harm's way."

"Dutchie? You mean, as in Dutch?" Tammie said.

Aurore shrugged weakly. "It was Connie's nickname for me. A silly childhood game we used to play. I was the duchess, your mother was the princess and Eleanor was the countess. The nickname stuck."

"You were the one who sent that letter to my mother."

Aurore stood frozen in place.

"How about we get beyond all the lies and start telling the truth to each other about what's really going on?" Dylan said.

Trudie nodded, her hands fisted at her chest. "It's time, Aurore. This has gotten too big for us to handle on our own."

Aurore pressed her hands to her face. "You know what will happen—"

"It's already happening!" Trudie cut in. "It's way out of control. One of them or both will be killed in the process, and I know you don't want that."

A deep sob tore away from Aurore's throat. "Oh, the day

Byron Davco befriended those fiends… There's been nothing but bloodshed and tears since."

"Tell me," Dylan insisted, advancing toward Aurore. "Whose bloodshed?"

Serena was still sobbing, her face covered and her head buried against Tammie's shoulder. It was hard to hear over her cries.

"Eleanor Davco's death was no accident," Trudie said, tears filling her eyes. "She was murdered by the very people who have haunted this family for years."

"Aztec Corporation?" Dylan said.

Aurore's eyes widened. "You know about them?"

"Enough to know Cash learned about them and they're here in this town right now."

Aurore began to pace and shook her head. "They said they'd kill the baby. I didn't know what else to do."

Serena's sobs increased, and Tammie shushed her as best she could. "What baby?" she asked.

"My baby!" Serena sobbed, then threw her head back and cried harder. The rest of her words were muffled. *"They stole my baby!"*

THIRTEEN

The living room crackled with tension. Wide-eyed, Dylan took in the faces of the people in the room. "Serena and Cash had a baby? I'm assuming this baby is Cash's child?"

Aurore's face showed resignation and distress. "She is."

"She's a beautiful little girl," Trudie said. "Looks just like her daddy."

"Ellie. Serena named her after Eleanor," Aurore said, looking straight at Tammie.

Trudie put a hand over her mouth to stifle a sob and pulled Serena into an embrace. "You poor child. You've been through so much."

Aurore continued to pace the room. "We didn't mean to let it get this far. We didn't know what else to do. When Byron became so ill, it all went to pieces."

"Why don't you start by telling us the truth?"

He thought of the Bible verse about the truth setting you free. He'd waited for this moment, and so had Tammie. And yet, he already had a deeper understanding of Cash and why he'd kept the truth from him.

Dylan couldn't sit. There were too many emotions

running through him. His brother was a father, and *he* was an uncle. It wasn't just about his brother's life anymore. It was about a little baby who was his kin.

In the quiet room, fear struck him. He looked at everyone and saw that they were all silent, as if everyone were waiting for someone else to make the first move.

"Tell me what happened to the baby," Dylan said as anxiety rose up his spine.

"They took Ellie!" Serena cried. Her sobs were more under control now, making it easier to understand her words.

Tammie stroked her sister's head. "Tell me what happened, Serena," Tammie asked. "Who did this?"

Aurore nervously played with her hands, as if she were wringing out a wet towel. "Byron Davco was a prominent businessman in his early days. It was what drew Eleanor to him. Of course, she had always come from money and he, well…he was a poor child who'd made good after coming home from Vietnam. He'd gone to college and made a name for himself."

"What went wrong?" Tammie asked.

She stopped pacing. "He got greedy. Oh, he loved Eleanor, but the fact that she had come from money always made him uncomfortable." She swept her hand to take in the room. "He enjoyed what money could bring, but he always felt like he needed more, as if he needed to prove to Eleanor that he could provide for her as much as her daddy did. I wonder if he ever really knew Eleanor at all.

"Eleanor was never one for looking at pretty clothes and fancy things. She looked at a person's heart and decided whether they were worth the friendship. We were friends since the cradle, Eleanor and I, and I never once felt her money got in the way. She was good people."

Trudie continued. "But Byron never got over being poor. It was as if he felt unworthy, even with all that money in the bank. That's why it was easy for Manuel Turgis to seduce him with the idea of more money."

She turned to Dylan. "Until about ten years ago, Manuel Turgis was a high-ranking executive in Aztec Corporation."

"So far, everything my contact in Chicago has managed to uncover about Aztec Corporation has been legit," Dylan said. He didn't mention that his contact was his sister. Suddenly he wondered if all the poking around she'd done would somehow get back to the people at Aztec.

"And it would be," Aurore said. "To the Colombian government, the head of Aztec Corporation might as well be royalty. And because of that, their illegal dealings are overlooked."

Tammie looked at Dylan and then Aurore. "Drugs?"

Trudie laughed with disgust. "That's not the half of it. It's more than just drugs, although I'm sure that yields them a hefty bonus."

"Then what?" Tammie added.

"Stolen artifacts. The real stuff," Serena said, pulling away from Trudie and running to the statue Dylan had seen the other day. She picked it up and smashed it on the floor. "This is what was so precious to them that they took my family away from me."

"I don't understand. I thought those were reproductions," Tammie said.

It finally dawned on Dylan. "That one might be, but I'm guessing not all of them are."

"You're right," Aurore said. "They use the auctions as a cover to move stolen art of all kinds and sell them on the black market. Byron used to be a middleman to help them launder the money into foreign bank accounts. For a while it worked for him. But then Eleanor got suspicious."

"She always did have a nose for sniffing out the truth," Trudie said, then looked at Tammie and chuckled. "You're a whole lot like her."

"How do you know?"

"Your mother always spoke of you. It did her heart good to see you grow up a beautiful woman like Eleanor."

"You knew my mother, too? Connie Gardner?"

"Eleanor's dad used to call the four of us peas in a pod. Where there was one, there were the other three. It broke my heart to lose Eleanor, and then to lose Connie, too, when she left. But the friendship always remained. I watched you grow up from afar, with the pictures your mom and dad sent. It wasn't often enough. We were careful to make sure not to attract attention."

"Did Cash find out about these stolen artifacts?" Dylan said.

"He did," Aurore said, "but it isn't as simple as that."

"What about you and Cash?" Dylan asked Serena. She appeared much more in touch with reality than she had been in days. She was more like she'd been the day they arrived in Eastmeadow.

"What do you mean?" Serena asked, her bottom lip wobbling with emotion. Her eyes were red from crying. The skin around them was puffy. But she was looking at him, really looking at him, for the first time.

"Pastor Robbins said you two were close."

Serena rolled her eyes slightly and shook her head. "Your brother wasn't just a man I had a child with, Dylan. He was my husband."

The room went silent for a moment. How was it possible that Cash had a wife and he'd never known? And a child? Wouldn't he have told him something like that? Made his family a part of their life?

As if reading his expression, Serena added, "It hurt him deeply to keep the secret. You have no idea. He did it for our safety. I know all about you. Cash spoke of his family often. He loved you all so much."

"Then why didn't he ever trust us enough to tell us he was married?" He didn't expect an answer. Still stunned from the news, he dropped down into a chair and scrubbed his hand over his face.

"It wasn't because he didn't trust you. It was because he didn't know if Turgis would go after one of you. He did it to protect you."

"He knew about Manuel Turgis?"

"He was my husband. Of course he did. He knew it all, because I'd confided in him. Although we kept our marriage secret and very rarely went out in public together, especially after my father got so sick, we didn't keep secrets from each other."

Dylan leaned forward in the seat. "What happened when Byron got sick?"

Serena looked at Aurore, who nodded and walked to a cabinet, opening a drawer and pulling out a thick envelope. The paper was worn with creases, and smudged fingerprints stained the outside, showing it had been handled a lot.

"What is that?" Tammie asked.

"It's a letter from your father to Serena," Aurore said, handing it to her. "Byron knew he didn't have much time. His illness struck him fast. He needed Serena to finally know what happened so she could carry on what needed to be done."

"Which was?"

"Byron got in over his head," Aurore said. "Eleanor had her suspicions, but nothing she could ever put her finger on."

Trudie motioned with her head toward the portrait of Eleanor and a young Serena with disdain. "He'd insisted Eleanor and Serena pose for that enormous thing. Eleanor hadn't wanted to do it while she was pregnant." Then Trudie laughed. "What woman wants to have a constant reminder of how big she got during pregnancy?"

"But he was relentless," Aurore added. "He kept at her. She'd wanted to wait until Tammie was born, so she could have both her babies with her. But he wouldn't let up, and so she finally agreed."

"I don't get it," Tammie said, shaking her head in confusion. "Why would a portrait matter?"

Dylan rose from the chair. "I'm guessing it wasn't the portrait. It was the artist. Am I right?"

Trudie nodded. "It gave Byron a reason to do business with the artist and help Aztec Corporation hide stolen artwork. There was a series of paintings that had been stolen from a private collection. It was worth a fortune back then. I can only imagine what those paintings would be worth in today's dollars."

Aurore sat down. "Turgis needed a way to get the stolen painting to his buyer without there being a paper trail connecting him to it. He needed to hide it in case it fell into the wrong hands."

"How'd he do it?" Dylan asked.

Trudie huffed. "He had this artist paint over the original. Then they hung it out at the auction for everyone to see. Of course, the price tag on the painting was ridiculously high by normal standards, and no one bought it—which they expected—so they packed it up and shipped it out like they do a lot of goods sold. Except this one had already been bought and paid for. We're talking about millions of dollars here."

Dylan pulled out the postcard Sonny had couriered to him overnight. It was the one he'd seen at Cash's apartment. He looked at the picture.

"Is this one of them?" he asked.

"Looks like it." Trudie sneered. "It'd been in the papers a few years back, when the painting supposedly emerged from hiding."

"If the paintings were shipped out, what was the problem? Why is Turgis after the Davcos?" Tammie asked.

"The money had changed hands. The buyer had put the funds into a foreign bank account, waiting for the painting to be shipped. Only that's when Eleanor found out. The final transaction never went through." Aurore broke down and wept then, turning her face away from them until she could contain herself. "Eleanor got ahold of Byron's paperwork and wouldn't let him have it."

Trudie's face turned hard with anger. "Eleanor fought bitterly with Byron to stop. She feared her babies would be hurt somehow. You don't underestimate people like this."

"High-level Colombian cartel disguised as businessmen," Dylan said, mimicking the words Matt had used on the phone earlier.

Trudie raised an eyebrow. "You *have* done your home-work, young man."

Dylan pressed on. "Tell me what else happened."

"Eleanor was so upset. She was almost to term. The night of the fi— That night, she'd packed her bags and told Byron she was leaving him. Of course, he begged her not to go. He became—" Trudie glanced briefly at Serena "—enraged," she said, almost apologetically.

Serena's eyes widened. "My father?"

"You were too young, child. That night changed him. Eleanor threatened to go to the authorities. She was desperate at that point, and she refused to give him the paperwork that had the numbers to the foreign bank account. Looking back, I almost wish she had. She'd still be alive today."

"What about the fire?" Tammie asked.

"Turgis set it," Trudie said. "He'd threatened Byron, beat him nearly senseless. He'd…threatened to kill Byron's family. But Byron insisted he'd pay back the debt if it was the last thing he did."

Aurore stood still, folding her arms across her chest as if she were cold. "He did, you know. Byron finally had the fortune he'd always hoped for, but it wasn't enough. He'd made Turgis look like a fool to his people. There's no price on that. The only thing that kept Byron alive was Turgis's greed. He made Byron pay back the money tenfold, taking all the profits from his business, which was much more than the original money for the painting. He wanted to ruin Byron, not only in business, but in his life. The money in Eleanor's trust took care of the house and Serena's expenses, but all of Byron's money went to Turgis. He'd gotten quite crafty at fixing the books to show there was no profit from the company."

"You said Turgis started the fire? Why? If he was content to get his money from Byron, why would he set the fire?" Dylan asked.

Aurore looked at Trudie, then turned away. Trudie spoke next, her voice thick with emotion. "You can break a man's legs and arms, you can torture him until he can't stand any more. But nothing is more torturous than taking what is most precious to him. Turgis had intended to kill Eleanor and the baby that night. It was his revenge. Byron knew it, and came rushing home to get them. He begged Eleanor one more time to give him the paperwork with the foreign account, and I think she might have conceded, only she was so upset, she went into labor. Tammie came so quickly, there wasn't time to call for help.

"In those few hours before the fire, Eleanor confided only in the tight-knit circle she knew she could trust. Me and Aurore—" she looked at Tammie "—and Connie. We promised we'd take care of you both, and we've done the best we could."

Tammie had been reading the letter from Byron Davco to Serena, tears filling her eyes. "He knew he was losing his battle with Alzheimer's when he wrote this."

"Yes," Serena said. "He told me about you. He even showed me pictures of you that Connie sent."

"When Serena turns thirty years old, she'll be able to do as she pleases with the money Eleanor had set up in trust. Your father urged her to give it all to Turgis—the house, the money, everything. It's the family fortune, but Turgis wants it all. He'd never hurt Serena, because she holds the key to the money. But anyone connected with her is fair game."

Serena started to cry again. "That's why he took my Ellie."

"And Cash?"

Aurore shook her head. "When they took the baby, Cash was beside himself. He went after Turgis. With his work in the DEA, he knew these people. He'd already been arrested on that drug trafficking charge, but he didn't care. He's quite a brave man."

Dylan couldn't have agreed more. But the word *stupid* came to mind, as well. Why hadn't he asked for help? This was too big for him to tackle alone. But he could see Cash walking through fire, fueled by his love for his wife and his baby, if it meant he could save them.

"How'd they get to the baby?" Dylan asked, pacing, unable to sit.

"That's just it. No one knows."

He swung around and looked at the women in the room. "What do you mean, no one knows? You have to have some idea how they did it. Was the baby ever alone?"

"Never." Serena shook her head. "Cash didn't want us to leave the house."

"And there were no signs of a break-in?" Tammie asked.

Aurore shook her head. "I don't know how they're getting into the house. Byron had a security system put in place years ago. If he could have afforded an armed guard, he would have done that, as well. But it's not the only time. Every so often, one of these statues appears, here in the living room."

Tammie's eyes widened. "What do you mean appears?"

"Just that. It isn't there when we go to bed, but it's there when we wake up."

Realization showed on Tammie's face. "That's why you wanted me to lock the bedroom door at night."

Aurore sighed bitterly. "Not that it would have helped. Turgis seems to have men everywhere."

"Why did Connie and Aaron take Tammie?" Dylan asked.

Trudie closed her eyes and stood. "I can barely stand the memory of it. Eleanor called me. The stress must have brought labor on early. I raced right over, while Aurore helped her deliver Tammie in the upstairs bedroom.

"Byron had already fled with Serena and brought her to the church. Aurore met me outside, with Tammie in her arms. I brought her right to Connie and Aaron. They knew they had to leave right then, leave everything they had, or Turgis would kill Tammie, too. It made sense for Connie to take Tammie. They had no children of their own. It was easier that way. Meanwhile, Aurore had gone back into the house to help Eleanor, but the fire was already out of control."

Tears rained down Aurore's cheeks, and she could hardly speak. "She was so weak, she could barely move. I tried to pick her up and help her, but when the smoke became too thick, she begged me to leave her, to save myself. She made me promise I'd take care of the babies, and I've dedicated my life to keeping that promise.

"This whole room was engulfed with flames and the exits were blocked." She touched her face. "It was so hot, I almost didn't make it. I ended up running through the tunnel out back. By that time, the fire department had arrived, but it was too late to save Eleanor."

Tammie pointed to the portrait on the wall. "How did the portrait survive the fire?"

"It had only been delivered the day before the fire, and it was in the barn with a bunch of other paintings Byron had waiting to ship. The fresh paint made Eleanor nauseous. She'd wanted to air it out before putting it up. Byron treasured it. He said it was the only thing he had left of his beloved wife and his baby girl."

"Where's this tunnel?" Dylan asked.

Aurore waved a hand. "It's gone now. It was part of the original structure, a way for the servants to get to the barn in bad weather. The original mansion dated back to the late 1700s. It was one of the first homes in Eastmeadow. Most of the older homes had tunnels to the barns so servants could take care of the animals. After the fire, it was destroyed."

"Are you sure?"

"Positive. The opening was cemented shut after the fire and the tunnel was filled in. There's nothing but an ugly sc—" Aurore touched her face. "There's a black scar on the wall in the basement now."

Tammie handed Dylan the letter. "Why would Turgis come after the family after all this time? If he's been quiet—"

"Oh, he was never quiet. Never!" Aurore said. "He took pleasure in taunting Byron, reminding him what a fool he'd made of both of them."

"Daddy made yearly payments to Turgis. It wasn't payment for the money that was lost. It was in exchange for our safety," Serena said. "Yours and mine."

"Manuel Turgis is a greedy man. It was never enough." Aurore paused. "Then Byron got sick."

When Aurore couldn't go on, Trudie continued. "He

was going fast, and he knew it." She motioned to the letter in Dylan's hands.

"When was that?" Dylan asked.

"Two or three years ago. Maybe a little longer. His business started to falter. He lost control of it and could no longer manipulate the books to his advantage. That's when the payments stopped."

Tammie was quiet. Dylan could see the wheels in her head spinning.

"My parents knew this?" she asked.

Trudie nodded. "I called your mom. You'd just finished college and moved to Vancouver. Since you weren't in Winchester with them, we all thought you were safe."

"Until the boat explosion," Tammie said.

No one said a word, but the message was clear.

Tammie looked at each of them one by one. "Turgis was behind the boat explosion, wasn't he?"

"I can't be certain," Aurore said, a look of sympathy in her eyes.

Trudie added, "He's a very powerful man. He manages to stay under the radar of the law here in the U.S."

Aurore threw up her hands in disgust. "He's considered a hero in Colombia. There are those who wish they could run him out, but no one will cross him for fear of what he'll do."

Tammie sat silent. She could barely remember the explosion, but it was still in the back of her mind. She could almost feel the physical pain of it.

She wanted Dylan to come to her, to tell her the pain would go away, tell her she was safe and make her feel like she'd felt in the church that day. But it would be a lie. He could guarantee none of that. And she knew he wouldn't lie to her.

He was standing across the room, looking at her. For a moment, he looked helpless, but then his face turned hard.

"He hasn't met me yet," Dylan said.

"What? Don't be foolish like your brother, young man. You don't know what you're up against. I don't care how many years you've spent in the military."

"I'm not going to be foolish. But I'm not going to lay down and die, either. If Turgis is the reason my brother and his baby are missing, then I'm going to find him and I'm going to find my family."

"At what cost?" Aurore said.

"Do you think you've done better here?" Dylan asked her. "Drugging Serena to keep her quiet? Keeping Tammie away from her family her whole life?"

"We did what we had to do."

"Well, it wasn't enough!" His anger had gotten the best of him, and Tammie could see that he knew it. Dylan closed his eyes, as if the realization of what was happening to his brother hit him. Colombian gangsters weren't kind, and Tammie guessed he had a clear image in his head of what might have happened.

Dylan had spent years in the military. He'd probably seen more horrors than Tammie could ever imagine. He knew that if Cash had gotten in over his head with people like Turgis, there was no reason for them to spare his life.

FOURTEEN

The stair creaked beneath Tammie's bare feet as she quietly took each step down. She didn't bother to look at the portrait of her mother. *Eleanor.* The painting haunted her.

She should be falling-down tired, giving in to sleep. But her emotions were at war with each other. One part of her told her to run, that nothing here was safe. Another told her she had no choice but to stay and fight to the end. She wondered if her parents had felt that way when they made the decision to leave with her.

She hadn't left the house for two nights. Aurore had invited Dylan to stay at the house, rather than at the campground. It made sense. Even though no one had said anything, Tammie knew they all felt safer with him here. She certainly did.

In the past two days, Dylan had been in constant communication with his sister and his contacts in Chicago, trying to get more information they could use to find Cash and Ellie. As he did, Tammie would look at Dylan from across the room when he was busy talking on the phone. It was hard to imagine that she hadn't known him just a few short days ago. It seemed as if he'd always been here with her.

In the evenings, when it was quiet, she'd sit with him

in the living room and he'd hold her. Despite the seriousness of what they were facing, he remained lighthearted during those moments. She loved his laugh, and the stories he told about his brother and sister.

Every once in a while, when he got quiet, she'd turn to look at him and see the pain on his face. A quick kiss and hug were enough to erase it. At least for the time being.

As she walked through the house, the moon shone bright through the large picture window and the French doors at the back of the living room, giving Tammie a clear view of the backyard. Slowly, she moved toward the window, only to be startled by the large, dark form sitting back in a wing chair that faced the backyard.

"Dylan, you scared me," she said, putting her hand over her heart.

"Did I? I didn't think anyone was awake."

His voice was low, but seemed to boom in the quiet room.

"What are you doing up?" he asked.

"The same as you, I suppose."

Tammie didn't have to see his face to know how the day had worn him down. He was slumped back in a large chair that overlooked the garden that Sam Watson had so painstakingly taken care of.

He opened his arms for her to sit with him. There wasn't much room in the wing chair, so she sat on his lap, and he immediately wrapped his arms around her as she rested her head on his shoulder. The world didn't seem as scary when he was holding her like this.

"Do you think they're still alive?" she asked, her voice cracking. They hadn't spoken of it and yet, somehow, she knew that was what Dylan was thinking of now.

"I don't know," he answered. "I pray they are. But I know what we're dealing with here, and that doesn't make me feel all warm and fuzzy inside."

"My heart breaks for Serena. To lose both of them…" Tammie bit her lip, tried to compose herself.

Unable to sit, she lifted herself to her feet, out of Dylan's embrace, and walked to the window. The night was still. Not even a stray cat was scurrying outside in the yard.

"It'll never be over, will it?" she said, finding her voice again. "Manuel Turgis will never leave this family alone. I've only lived with this for two days, and already I can't stand it."

Dylan came up behind her. She was wearing a heavy terrycloth robe that probably made her look like a big polar bear, but vanity was the furthest thing from her thoughts. Her sister's baby was missing. Her sister's husband, Dylan's brother, had gone after the baby. He'd walked right into the lion's den to fight the beast, and the chances of finding them at all, never mind alive, were low.

Dylan's gentle hands on her shoulders made her want to weep all over again. But instead of saying a word, Dylan remained still behind her with his arms draped around her shoulders, allowing Tammie to take the same comfort she'd felt earlier.

She leaned back against him, felt a connection that wrapped around her like a lifeline. Without words, she placed her hand over his, letting him know how much his comfort meant to her.

Two hands connected. Wasn't that what life was about? A merging of souls through love. It startled her to even think of it, but she knew that was where she was headed with Dylan. He'd touched her heart so deeply by just being…Dylan. His strength and his love of family showed with every breath he took.

And he'd taken her care into his hands, as well. His faith in the Lord gave her a peace that she hadn't felt in a long time.

Oh, what it would be like to wrap herself in the strength that he had, to feel that safe and secure? And yet, part of her wanted desperately to tell him to run. Run as far as he could, away from her and the pain being with her could bring.

"You've got a lot spinning in that head of yours," he said, breaking into her thoughts.

"I've forgiven my parents. They did what they had to do. I just wonder if I can ever forgive myself."

He turned her around to look at him. "What are you talking about?"

"I doubted them. That I could ever doubt their love for me, even for a second, is horrible." A tear slid down her cheek. "My parents were killed because of me, Dylan."

"You can't think that way."

"Oh, but I can. All this time, I've been so angry with them for not telling me the truth."

"It's hard not to question something that seems so unfair."

"Yes, I know. But the truth is, they put their lives on the line for me. It was because of me that they died."

"Manuel Turgis is responsible for their deaths, Tammie. Not you."

She shook her head. "I know it was nothing I did intentionally and it wasn't in my control. But the fact remains, Turgis was targeting me that day we were supposed to leave on that boat trip. Not my parents. It's only by the grace…the grace of God that I didn't make it to the boat on time, that the captain decided to fuel the tanks while waiting for me to arrive. If I hadn't been late—"

"You'd be dead, too."

The abrupt remark hit her as hard as Dylan had meant it to. He'd shocked her. Wide-eyed, she looked up at him.

"Don't you see the crime in *that*, Tammie?" he said, his voice low and steeped with emotion. "I can't stand the thought that they could have succeeded in ending your life, too. Of never having had you in my life. Of never having had the opportunity to hold you in my arms."

He pulled her into a tight embrace, and she closed her eyes, allowing the tears to fall.

"Don't say that, Dylan."

"Why not? It's what I feel."

"Then you need to stop. Don't you see that whatever it is we've been feeling can't go anywhere?"

"Too late. It's a done deal."

He put his arms loosely around her, allowing her to flee if she wanted. But she held fast, resting her hands on his shoulders. Though her heart was in turmoil, she had to see this through.

"My parents spent their life protecting me from something I didn't even know existed, raising me without the fear they must have had the entire time I was growing up. They died because of me."

"And you think that's going to happen to me?"

"Yes."

"You're wrong."

Tammie shook her head. "You don't know that. Manuel Turgis and his cohorts have hurt too many people. Fear has kept Serena from living a normal life, from being able to love her husband and raise her baby without fear. These people don't care who they hurt."

"I don't care what kind of threats they pose, Tammie."

She pulled out of his arms. "Well, I do. It's because of the threat they could hold over me that my parents died. I won't let them hurt you."

"I don't want to lose you."

She covered her face with her hands. "Don't you see? What kind of life could we ever have living under the threat that Aztec Corporation and Manuel Turgis has held over this family? So what if Serena pays Turgis the entire family fortune? That doesn't mean it will end. You know that."

"I can't just walk away, Tammie." He reached down and kissed her mouth, letting his lips linger on hers, resting his hand at the nape of her neck. When he pulled away, he left his hand in place and looked deeply into her eyes. "I've never been more sure of anything in my life."

"Do you want to live your life like Serena and Cash? Do you want to worry about what might happen every time we walk out the door? I don't. I don't want to look into a stranger's face and wonder if that person means me harm or not. I have to live with that, but you don't have to. You can walk away from it right now."

"If you believe that, then I don't know where you've been these last few days. Whether you wish it or not, I do have to live with this. Because the day I met you on that street is the day I stopped thinking about my life as being just about me and what I want." She looked at his face and saw the raw emotion there.

"Yeah, that's right," he said. "And I can't believe that you're not thinking that very same thing."

"That's a luxury I won't allow myself," she said, turning away from him.

What Tammie had seen in Dylan was something she'd longed for without even knowing it. He was the kind of man that made her think of a lifetime together. He held the principles and faith that matched her own.

But Tammie wouldn't go there. There was too much at stake.

"Why won't you just walk away from me, while you still have the chance to have a normal life?"

He closed his eyes. "Because I can't. For the first time I feel like there's something more to wake up to every day than just me. I used to think that being a Marine was enough. And for a long time, it was. But family is important. I know that with all my heart, and for me that starts with you."

He tilted her chin up to look at him.

"How can that be? If we allow our relationship to go any further, there'll be no going back. What if we end up married?"

He smiled. "That's a nice thought."

She shook her head. "How can you say that? Any children we may have together will be a target for Manuel Turgis. You know that. What kind of life would we have if we had to hide like Serena has done her whole life? I don't know how my parents were able to stand it."

"Then we don't hide. I'm all for getting right in Turgis's face if I have to. I mean to make some noise, Tammie, and I mean to tell him that as of right now every single member of this family is not going to stand for it anymore."

"This hasn't stopped for nearly thirty years. What makes you think they'll stop coming after us?"

His eyes glinted with a hardness that would have frightened her if she didn't know it wasn't directed at her.

"Let them. I want them to come after us. And I want them to know that I'm coming after them. I want them to know this family is not going to run and hide."

She wrapped her arms around him and held tight.

"That's right, Tammie. You just stay here in my arms. It'll be all right."

"I can't do this, Dylan. I just can't let you do this." Tammie pulled away and backed up slowly. Then she ran from the room and up the stairs.

"Tammie?" he called after her. But she didn't turn around, and he didn't follow.

Instead, he stood rooted in place as he watched Tammie disappear into the darkness. He could barely see her as she moved, but his eyes searched until he could no longer see movement at all.

Sitting back down in the chair by the window, he closed his eyes and prayed. There'd been many nights when he was out on an op that had gone bad and he thought for sure he'd be leaving this earth to join God in heaven. Prayer had always been the glue that kept him together. Faith was the beam of light that showed him the way through even his darkest hours.

"I know I've asked a lot of You these last few weeks, Lord, but I'm asking for Your guidance again," he said in the stillness of the room. "Please don't let me be blinded by how I feel about this woman. I don't want to lose her. Show me the way to save her, Cash and my little niece from what threatens them. Or give me the strength to walk away, if that is what needs to be done to save them. As hard as it is, I won't question Your plan."

He sat in the darkness as the tears came. His heart swelled with emotion that he hadn't allowed himself to feel.

Fear. Love. Hate. They were all mingled into one.

Aztec Corporation was big enough to get lost inside. From what Sonny had uncovered, it was a tangled mess that led to no one in particular. It was a smart way to keep people from discovering those really responsible for the art thefts. And it made it almost impossible to know where to start to find who took the baby or how to find Cash.

He wouldn't let up, Dylan thought. He'd fought for clarity. He'd asked God to help him find the right way, to give him strength. Inside, he felt it growing stronger and stronger. Not born of anger, but of resolve.

Aztec Corporation had already taken his beloved brother and the niece he had never even known existed before he came here. He wasn't going to let them take the only woman he'd ever truly cared for. And he did care deeply for Tammie. It almost amazed him that in such a short time his feelings had grown the way they had.

Yeah, he was going to make some noise, all right. And he knew just where to start.

FIFTEEN

The morning had come much too early, Tammie thought as she pulled herself out of bed. To say that she felt as if a Mack truck had run her over would have been an understatement.

She felt worse.

After a quick shower that did little to rouse her more, she pulled on a favorite pair of jeans and an oversized college sweatshirt. Her hair needed serious attention, but she didn't give it anything beyond putting it in a clip in the back of her head.

Serena had been quiet last night. Too exhausted to cry any more for her baby and her husband, she'd slept through the night, even without a sedative to calm her.

After pulling her sneakers on, Tammie decided to check on Serena to see if she was up to eating breakfast. As tired as Tammie was, she couldn't sleep. She didn't feel much like eating, either, but she could make pancakes and toast for whoever was up. Serena needed to keep up her strength, especially now.

Tammy stood at the top of the stairs and listened for movement downstairs. She didn't hear any, and figured everyone else must be still asleep.

As she turned and walked back toward the bedrooms, she thought of the way Dylan had held her last night, making her feel as if everything he said were possible. That he could fight against the seemingly invisible threat of Aztec Corporation, that they could be together without fear.

Oh, how she wanted to believe him. But how could she, if the very man responsible for bringing this cruelty to his family hadn't been able to?

She opened the door to Serena's room and walked inside, pausing only long enough to notice that the door wasn't locked. The blankets on the bed were disheveled, but the bed was empty.

"Serena?" she said quietly, walking toward the bathroom. The door was open. A tube of toothpaste lay uncapped on the vanity. A hairbrush had fallen into the sink instead of being put in its place. Two white towels were crumpled on the floor by the tub.

She swung around, toward the door, listening to see if she could hear Serena. Nothing.

Quickly, she ran to the stairs and descended them. Serena had to be somewhere in the house. Perhaps Tammie had slept longer than she thought.

When she got downstairs, she saw Dylan stretched out on the sofa in the living room. He hadn't slept in the room Susan had set up for him.

His eyes were closed, and his dark, thick hair was sticking up against the stark white pillowcase. He reminded Tammie of a little boy. But she knew he was so much stronger and more powerful than that.

Dylan had urged her not to give up on him, to pray for them to find a way out of this. But he'd also said he was going after the people responsible for doing them all harm. That meant Manuel Turgis. She couldn't bear to think of what harm would come to Dylan if he knocked heads with the Colombian gangster.

Pulling herself away from the sight of him, she moved toward the kitchen and pushed through the swinging door. The first time she'd been in the kitchen of the mansion was the day Serena had thrown the dinner tray. Susan had always been a little protective of the kitchen, telling her she wasn't doing her job right if Tammie felt the need to feed herself.

Tammie wasn't so easily intimidated now. The kitchen was quiet, but a scraping sound drew her toward the basement door. The door was cracked open an inch. Curious, Tammie opened it, just enough to listen for noise. Someone was downstairs.

"Aurore?" she called quietly.

No one responded.

Flipping the switch on the wall, she was greeted by a harsh light. She shielded her face only for a moment, until her eyes adjusted.

As cellars go, this was one of the mustiest, Tammie thought as she descended the stairs. Remnants of the long-ago fire were evident in places on the charred stone walls.

Noise was coming from the far end of the basement. Tammie moved between boxes that were piled up to the ceiling, keeping her from seeing what was causing the scraping against concrete.

"Susan? Aurore?" she called out, but got no answer. "Is that you?"

In the far corner stood a tall cabinet. None of the cans and boxes that filled its shelves seemed to have been disturbed. Yet the cabinet sat strangely askew to the wall, and the fingerprints in the dust on the cabinet showed it had been recently touched. Tammie quickly moved toward the sound she heard in that direction.

What she found shocked her. Behind the cabinet was an opening the size of a small doorway, just large enough for her to get through. Stones that had made up the wall had been knocked out, leaving a jagged opening that she had to crouch to fit into. The walls around the doorway were charred and still smelled like old ash. It made her skin crawl, but she pressed on.

She looked back toward the opening to the basement and wondered if she should get Dylan. He'd be angry with her for going down here alone. She could almost hear him scolding her about being careful. But behind that concern, there'd be warmth in his eyes. Warmth and concern that spoke of his feelings for her.

But he'd been sleeping so peacefully that she didn't want to wake him if this turned out to be a false alarm. Besides, whoever was down here might be gone. She moved down the narrow tunnel. Aurore had said that this was how she'd escaped during the fire. Obviously she'd been mistaken about it being sealed off.

This had to be how the people from Aztec Corporation had been able to move unnoticed into the house and kidnap little Ellie. How no one in the house could have known this was still here was beyond Tammie's comprehension.

A door at the end of the tunnel slammed closed.

"Who's there? Serena, is that you?"

There was only a sliver of light behind Tammie that gave any light at all in the tunnel. But Tammie didn't need much to recognize the person who came into view.

"Susan?"

"You shouldn't be down here, Tammie."

"I was just thinking the same about you," she said.

It was then that Tammie noticed the shovel in Susan's hand. She gasped, filling her lungs with musty dirt, and gauged the distance to the door she'd come through in the basement. She could make a run for it. Scream for help. If Aurore was in the kitchen, surely she'd hear. Maybe Dylan would hear.

"All this time, it was you. You took little Ellie," Tammie said, keeping her eye on Susan.

"She's safe. She's being well taken care of."

Relief washed over Tammie at the thought that her little niece was alive.

Tears stung Tammie's eyes. "Where is she? Where is my sister's baby?" she demanded.

"Does it matter? You're never going to see her. If you'd have stayed out of Serena's life, we could have dealt with this quietly. Now you and your boyfriend have ruined everything."

"Take whatever you want. Serena will give it all to you. Just return her baby," Tammie pleaded.

The sound of Susan's laughter was closer. Tammie inched her way back toward the basement, using the dirty walls as a guide in the dim light.

"Where is she? Tell me where the baby is!"

A scrape on the floor told Tammie that Susan was much too close. She turned toward the basement opening, ready to bolt. She'd only managed to take a few steps before her world turned to darkness.

SIXTEEN

"It didn't take long for you to get comfortable here," Aurore said, coming into the living room. "You're receiving packages now?"

Dylan had just finished folding the last blanket and dropping it on top of the pillow when she came into the room, holding a package in her hands.

"Sorry, I didn't hear the doorbell or I would have gotten it," he offered.

Aurore looked at the address on the package. "You will tell me if you find anything, won't you?"

"Too much has gone unsaid for too long. There's no reason to keep secrets now."

She nodded, handing him the package and leaving the room without another word.

He'd hated the look on Tammie's face last night, when she came into the living room. He recalled the way she'd looked as she stood by the window in the moonlight. Her beauty stole his breath away every time he looked at her. But last night, she'd looked haunted. If all it would take to keep her safe was to hold her in his arms, he'd surely do it. But he knew that wasn't enough.

How many missed opportunities had Aztec Corporation had to get to her? God had been with her that day the boat exploded. He'd spared her, and Dylan thanked Him for His mercy. Otherwise, Dylan would never have known Tammie, never have fallen in love with her. That seemed unimaginable now.

He'd prove her wrong, he'd decided last night as he tried to get comfortable on the sofa. Nothing about this house put his mind at ease. He'd been right to trust his gut instinct that Tammie shouldn't stay here. And yet, was she really safe outside these walls?

Dylan dropped down to the sofa and ripped the seam on the large envelope that had been couriered to the Davco mansion. His partner in Chicago had been his liaison with the computer system he was using to gather information about Aztec Corporation.

Sonny had been his eyes and ears on the other end, trying to find out how it all tied in with Cash. When he called her to tell her about Cash and the baby, she'd broken down and sobbed, but promised to relay the information to their parents so that he could continue to work on finding Cash and the baby.

He thought about what it must have been like for Sonny. It couldn't have been easy to tell his Mom and Dad about Cash and Serena's marriage. His parents were such traditional people that no doubt they'd been brokenhearted that Cash hadn't included them on such a joyous occasion. And then to learn they were grandparents, and that Ellie was missing, too. Part of him wished he'd been there to help Sonny break the news to them.

But leaving Tammie wasn't an option. She was a target,

as well, and the last thing Dylan was going to do was allow the hit men to get another chance at her.

Opening the envelope wide, he spilled the contents onto the coffee table and began to rifle through them. Matt had been quick with his search, for which he was grateful.

This is totally off the record, buddy, Matt had scribbled on the back of a computer-generated report. *You know Paulson will have my head if it makes it back to him I helped you on this.*

Captain Paulson hadn't been all that thrilled with Dylan taking leave or the reason for it. He'd be even less thrilled if he found out that Dylan had dragged a member of his department in on it.

He turned the computer paper over. The first pieces of paper were random police reports on the staff at the mansion. As he'd suspected, Sam Watson had a record for theft, but it was so far back in his youth he was sure Byron Davco had probably overlooked it—if he'd even known.

The second report was on Aurore. Nothing earth-shattering there. Not even a parking ticket. Just random information about her birth and place of residence. She had indeed lived in Eastmeadow her whole life.

The last one was empty. On the bottom, Matt had scribbled, *Thought this was* real *interesting. Who is she?*

"Certainly not who she says she is," Dylan muttered to himself.

He pulled out the file that Sonny had sent him yesterday. He'd managed to download it and read most of the contents, but today he was looking for something altogether different. He searched the photographs, mostly of Manuel Turgis at various functions in Colombia. Frustrated, he tossed the reports on the floor and spread the pictures out on the coffee table.

"Aurore?" he called out.

He recognized the face of one of the people in the picture. It wasn't a shot of Manuel Turgis, but rather a picture taken at an Aztec Corporation function. Sonny had circled the face of a man in the crowd, a Colombian businessman who'd been arrested for drug trafficking in the U.S. and extradited back to his native country to appear on charges he faced there. The picture barely showed the person standing about ten feet behind him. But now that Dylan knew what to look for, the face was unmistakable.

"Aurore?" he yelled, getting to his feet quickly.

He didn't wait for her to return his call. Instead, he pushed through the kitchen doors and found her standing by the stove, a teapot full of steaming water in her hand.

"Where's Serena?" he asked, still holding the picture.

"I assume she is in her room."

"And Susan?"

"I don't know. There are no plates in the sink, so she never brought Serena her breakfast. That's unlike her—"

He cut her off impatiently. "Have you seen Tammie this morning?"

"Isn't she still asleep?"

Dylan bolted from the kitchen, ran through the house and went up the stairs, taking them two at a time. He didn't know which door was the one to Tammie's room, so he opened every door in the hallway until he found the one that had her suitcase sitting by the bed.

"Tammie?" he called. The bed was unmade. Her bathrobe was flung across the rumpled blankets.

He looked around the room. The door to the bathroom was open, and he could see that she wasn't in there.

Aurore came running into the room, out of breath. "What's wrong?"

"Where's Susan? If she's not with Serena, where would she be?"

"I don't know. She usually tells me when she's going to leave the house. I assumed since she wasn't with Serena that she was doing laundry."

"Where is that, exactly?"

"The laundry room, through the kitchen."

"Is there access to the basement there?"

"No, just in the kitchen. Why?"

Dylan made his way down to the next bedroom door and pushed it open.

"The doors should be locked," Aurore said, her face filled with panic.

"Serena's not in her room."

As if she needed to see for herself, Aurore ran down the hall and into Serena's bedroom, checking the bathroom to see if she was inside.

"Serena! Oh, no, they've taken her!" she cried.

Dylan's feet were barely touching the stair treads as he raced downstairs, taking note of the large picture hanging on the wall.

Byron Davco had to have known his family was a target when he insisted Eleanor and Serena pose for that portrait. Serena had said he used to look at the picture and say it was all he had left of Eleanor and the child he never had a chance to love and raise.

He'd known, and yet he'd allowed this travesty to go on

all these years without seeking another way out. He'd allowed gangsters into his home, to bully and destroy his family, terrorizing them, threatening their safety. All the while, he'd kept them in danger instead of facing his mistakes head on and taking his punishment for his illegal dealings.

It wouldn't be Christian of Dylan to despise the man for his deeds when it was clear he'd also tried, albeit without success, to keep Tammie and Serena safe. If it were his family...

Dylan stopped at the foot of the stairs and turned to look up at the portrait of Eleanor Davco and Serena.

At the top of the stairs, Aurore demanded, "Tell me what's going on! What do you know?"

"How long has Susan been with you?"

Aurore thought about it impatiently and then said, "Seven, eight years now."

"Right after the statute of limitations was up."

"What?"

"Turgis isn't after the Davco money. He's after the last painting."

He raced through the kitchen and pulled the cellar door open. The basement light was on. The damp smell of old air and cement slapped him in the face. Aurore had said she'd used a secret tunnel from the basement to the barn to escape during the fire, but that it had been closed up when the mansion was rebuilt. Closed up at the time, yes. But that didn't mean it hadn't been dug out and rebuilt.

This house was big enough to work on at one end without someone hearing it being done on the other. Maybe that was the real reason Sam Watson had worked at night. Although nothing had come up in the report about him, that didn't mean Susan hadn't paid him off. Someone had to have been helping Susan move through the house unnoticed by Serena and Aurore. As drugged as Serena had been kept, it made sense that she hadn't heard any commotion.

But Aurore was another story. The woman's senses were as sharp as a knife. Only someone who was familiar to her could move through the house and manipulate her into thinking she was safe.

Fear clutched at him, rendering his legs nearly paralyzed as he moved down the cellar stairs, toward the darkness. Someone had turned the light to the cellar stairs on, but otherwise, the cellar was drenched in darkness, broken only by small slivers of light from the windows that hung high on the cellar walls.

Still, he moved. It wasn't about him or Cash now. It was about Tammie.

He'd been on many ops during his tours in the Marines. While there had been times he wasn't so sure he'd be coming home, the Lord had always kept him strong and he'd made it to see another sunrise. It was the same with him being a cop on the streets of Chicago. Some good men and women didn't make it home. A split decision that turned out to be wrong, or even a right one in the wrong circumstances, meant bad news for a loved one.

He'd always known the risks, and accepted them. God was with him, and if He decided it was his time to join Him, then so be it. Dylan had prayed and had made peace with that a long time ago. But the very thought of losing Tammie completely shut him down.

Dylan didn't have a gun with him, and even if he did, in this darkness he wouldn't have been able to make out what to shoot. He moved by instinct. His foot struck a box, and he stumbled. He put his hands out front to lead the way.

He'd just about decided to turn around and search outside when he heard a moan.

Heart racing, he moved through the darkness, searching the strange shadows with wide eyes until he found a figure on the floor. Relief shot through him as he dropped to the floor, but it was short-lived.

"Serena?" he said, turning her over. He couldn't see her face, but her eyes shone in what little light there was. They were rolled back in her head. "Serena, where is Tammie?"

She offered no response. She felt like dead weight in his hands, a sure indication that she'd been knocked out, either by force or by drugs. Hearing Aurore's footsteps on the stairs, he quickly laid her on the floor again and stood.

"Serena's back here!" he called out before moving toward a cabinet that looked out of place. And the dark shadows behind it.

The cement was cold and damp as he ran his hand up and down the doorway to see if he could find a light switch. Air from the basement seemed to be being sucked into the hole. He finally found a switch and turned it on.

The tunnel was long enough to reach what he assumed was the barn. It must have taken a long time to dig it out again without Aurore knowing. At the far end, a ladder was propped up against the wall. An opening above the ladder allowed natural light to spill into the space below.

Dylan took a few steps into the tunnel and stopped short, crouching down to look at a dark stain on the ground. He pressed his hand against the stain and felt wetness. When he brought his hand up to his nose, he thought he'd die. He knew the smell of this liquid all too well.

It was the smell of death.

Tammie's head felt as if it had been split wide open, like an overripe melon. As hard as she tried, she couldn't pry her eyes open. She was resting on something hard, with her legs pulled awkwardly to one side underneath her. Her back hurt from being in the odd position, so she tried to stretch out her legs to relieve the pain. But her feet were stuck, unable to move from where they were.

Somewhere outside of *wherever* she was, she heard voices. It was a woman, one who sounded strangely familiar, and two men. The woman sounded angry, but Tammie couldn't make out what she was saying. Suddenly the floor beneath her shifted and she was thrown to one side, knocking her arm and head against a hard wall.

"I told you to be careful!"

Susan? The wall she'd fallen against was made of wood. She felt the rough grain beneath her fingers as she moved her hand against it. What was Susan doing here?

Startled, she tried to move again, but her legs wouldn't budge. Panic rose up inside her like the swells of the ocean during a storm. It continued to build, even as realization hit that she was inside a box that was too small for her to stretch out.

Too weak to push against the walls, she was vaguely aware that she was being raised into the air. The voices sounded closer, but she couldn't hear much of what was being said above the banging of her pulse against her temple. Pain followed every throb.

Slowly, she reached her hand up and touched the spot that throbbed. She winced at the pain. Her hand came back wet and sticky.

The Lord will keep you from harm and safeguard your life, Tammie prayed silently. *He will guard your coming and going now and forevermore.*

Her stomach lurched with every movement of the wooden box. Bile rose up in her throat and stung the back of her mouth. Tammie braced her hands as best she could against the walls of the box, trying desperately to keep panic from taking over. She had to stay calm. She had to think of a way to save herself, or there was no chance of getting out of this alive.

"I'm sorry, Dylan," she whispered as tears stung her eyes. She'd pushed him away last night. He'd opened up to her, stood there with his emotions open and raw, and she'd pushed him away. What was worse, she hadn't opened up her heart to him and told him that she loved him. And she did. Of that she was certain.

The box suddenly twisted as if it were falling, making Tammie dizzy. Her head slammed against the wall again, and she was instantly plunged back into darkness.

SEVENTEEN

Dylan's Jeep was stuck in a cluster of cars. Main Street was littered with papers and debris, as if it were the day after the big Mardi Gras parade. Trucks were fighting for space, trying to load what furniture and antiques hadn't sold back onto their wagons so that they could head out to the next auction.

"It's a nightmare down here right now," the officer directing traffic said. "We're detouring everyone until after one o'clock today."

"I can't wait that long," Dylan said, and quickly filled him in on who he was and what had been happening down at the Davco mansion.

"I can't allow you in there without a police escort. I can't risk other people getting caught in the crossfire if it comes to that. Pull over to the side. We're waiting for backup."

"Tammie could be dead by the time the state police get here." Dylan ground out the words. "I'm not waiting."

The church's parking lot was empty. Dylan pulled his Jeep in and parked. The state police barracks were a good twenty minutes away. Susan could be long gone by then.

The police officer was still directing traffic around the

auction grounds, trying to calm dealers who were eager to get their goods out of town and on to the next auction.

Frustrated, Dylan climbed out of the Jeep and slammed the door shut. He was wasting precious time that Tammie might not have.

It wouldn't take him as long to navigate his way through the traffic on foot, but it might make getting away harder if Tammie was hurt when he found her.

And he *would* find her. He knew just where to start. By then, maybe backup from the state police would have arrived.

He rounded a corner and raced down a lane toward the area where he'd seen Aztec Corporation's tents. The landscape of the auction grounds had already changed, and the temporary landmarks he'd cataloged the other day to find his way around were no longer there.

Dylan spotted Susan, exactly where he'd suspected she'd be. She was sitting in the passenger side of a large truck that blended in with all the others that were lining the aisle. Two men were on the back of the flatbed, stacking crates and boxes.

At first, she didn't see him. But he didn't care if she did. In fact, he wanted to look her in the eye, let her feel cornered and scared, the way she'd made Serena feel all these years. All this time, Susan had been the vehicle on a path of destruction for both Serena and Cash. She'd been the one to take Ellie from the house through that tunnel and bring her God only knew where.

Before Dylan could even allow himself to think about the baby, he needed to find Tammie. She was here. He was sure of it. And if she was still alive, they were taking her with them.

Oh, please, God, let her still be alive. He couldn't lose her now.

Maybe it was better that the state cops hadn't arrived. They wouldn't be able to search for Tammie without a warrant. But Dylan could find probable cause before they came on the scene.

Cardboard boxes and wooden crates lined the aisles, waiting to be loaded on trucks. He ran through the aisles, staying behind other trucks and keeping an eye on Susan so that she wouldn't see him before he was ready. Given the sheer volume of crates, Dylan knew that looking for Tammie was going to be like looking for the proverbial needle in a haystack. For all he knew, Aztec Corporation could have already loaded a truck that was long gone.

Would they have had time to get Tammie out of here that quickly? He didn't know when she'd been taken or that she'd been taken here. But if Susan was here, in the open, it was a good bet Tammie was, too.

Dylan slowly moved around a smaller truck, trying not to rouse the suspicions of the Aztec crew.

Susan lifted her head, and her eyes widened when she spotted him. Sliding over to the driver's side of the truck, she gunned the engine and shifted into gear.

"Hey, whatcha doing?" one of the workers on the ground said, quickly moving out of the way to keep from getting flattened by the truck.

Hatred shone in Susan's bright eyes. He'd seen it in her before, but never this way, never with this purity that made her intentions so clear.

She revved the engine and beeped the horn once, signaling to her crew. "Forget the rest!" she yelled out the open window. "Let's go!"

"We're not done!" one worker said. He was still holding a box in his arms, but when he turned and saw Dylan running toward him with determination, he dropped it. "Let's roll!" he yelled, waving to his partner and jumping into the cab.

Dylan didn't move from the center of the lane. There were so many trucks littering the aisle that Susan would have to crash into them and then run him down to get away.

"Give it up, Susan!" he yelled.

He looked straight into her eyes, saw the contempt she held for him, and then ran toward the truck at full speed.

Tammie's eyes fluttered open at the sound of an engine whining close by. Her head ached, and she was finding it hard to make sense out of where she was. A small sliver of light shone through a tiny crack in the wood, but that was all the light she was afforded. Where was she? What had she been doing? She couldn't remember.

Suddenly, whatever she was resting on lurched forward. The enclosure she was trapped in bounced back and forth, knocking her arms and head against the sides.

She cried out once, closing her eyes against the white, blinding pain.

Dear Lord, save me! This couldn't possibly be the end. How could it be, when she'd only just found love? She'd never told Dylan she loved him. Even as they stood in the living room last night and it was clear that Dylan felt the same for her as she did for him, she hadn't uttered a word.

There had been no walls between them, and the emotion they felt for each other had been evident, even if the words hadn't been spoken.

She did love Dylan. It had hit her like a bolt of lightning hitting a mighty oak, slicing it in half. She was in love with Dylan. From the moment she'd met him, he'd dug under her skin, tearing away that protective layer she'd had to protect her from pain.

And then she heard his voice, and all she wanted to do was weep with relief. But at the same moment, realization collided with fear. If she was in danger, so was he!

"Dylan!" she called out. Her voice seemed muffled inside of the box.

The stench of exhaust fumes filled the tiny space she was in. She coughed and gasped, trying to pull fresh air into her lungs. But with every breath she took, the only air she got was poisonous exhaust.

Dylan's mind was made up. Susan wasn't getting away, even if she plowed that truck right over him. And he was counting on her wanting to do just that.

It might be Susan's intention to run him down, but if she thought she'd succeed, she was in for a big surprise. She'd let her hatred and her greed get in the way of her judgment, and Dylan knew he could use that to his advantage.

People were scurrying around him, yelling at him to get out of the way, as Susan shifted the truck into gear and advanced. But Susan had misjudged the width of the lane and the number of trucks on both sides. Dylan ran, quickly assessing the distance between an open flatbed truck in front of Beaumont's tent and the truck Susan was driving.

As she plowed forward, Dylan shifted right, climbing on top of the empty truck.

As he'd suspected she would, Susan veered toward the truck he was on, in an effort to knock him off. She was playing right into his hands. He held tight to the wood, and just as she rammed the truck, he leaped forward, jumping onto the running board and grabbing the steering wheel through the open window.

"Let go, you fool!" she yelled at him. But Dylan held tight against Susan's attempts to turn the steering wheel left, to bring the vehicle close enough to one of the other trucks to knock him off.

He was stronger, and managed to distract Susan just enough that he could turn the wheel to the right, sending the truck straight into a large boulder. Before the truck hit, he jumped from the running board and immediately tucked his body under to roll until he settled against a large crate of linens some yards away from where he'd jumped.

When he'd recovered from the impact of hitting the ground, he saw smoke seeping out of the hood of Susan's truck. The truck was a good twenty yards away from him. Within seconds, the small stream of smoke had turned into a black cloud that filled the air with fumes that stank. She wasn't going anywhere. At least not in that vehicle.

The man on the back of the truck jumped down. Even though he was unsteady on his feet, he ran through the tents and into a neighboring field that had been used as a make-shift parking lot for the auction. Dylan didn't pay him any mind. If the state police wanted to go after him, he'd let them. He wanted to make sure Susan stayed put.

He walked toward the truck and saw that Susan was holding her nose and blood was pouring down her shirt.

"Give it up, Susan!" he said when she fumbled with the ignition, trying to turn the engine over. "It's done!"

The man who'd climbed into the passenger's seat was knocked out, a spiderweb imprint on the windshield clearly marking the spot where he hit his head.

"You ruined everything!" she screamed as she abandoned her efforts to start the truck. "You're going to pay for this!"

In the background, Dylan heard the sound of sirens. The cavalry had arrived.

He climbed back up on the running board. "Where is she?"

"Find her yourself!" she spat back.

"Tell me where Tammie is!"

But Susan's eyes glazed over, and then rolled back as her head slumped back against the seat.

"No. Wake up!"

Dylan jumped down from the running board, keeping an eye on Susan while he assessed the area. If they were moving her and they wanted it to go unnoticed, they'd put her in a box or crate.

It took a minute for the dust to clear and the police officers to make their way down the lane toward the accident. As he waited, he searched the area, trying to figure out where Tammie might be. Heart pounding, he assessed his options until the officers were there. He immediately introduced himself to the state police and identified himself as a Chicago police officer.

"Did you find your girlfriend yet?" one officer asked.

The word *girlfriend* didn't quite seem right to Dylan. He didn't want a girlfriend. He wanted a wife, a life partner. He wanted Tammie to be that for him. He wanted to be a part of her life in a way he'd never wanted to share his life with a woman.

"No, but I'm guessing she's in one of those crates," he finally said.

The question of what Tammie was to him, what place she had in his life, was something he'd work out with her. And when he found her, he'd plead his case. No matter what danger was involved, no matter what kind of threat Manuel Turgis and his crew imposed, Dylan wasn't going to give up on Tammie and him. He was going to fight, and fight hard, to make Tammie see that they belonged together.

Three officers pulled Susan and the other man out of the truck. Susan was moaning with pain as blood ran down her face.

Dylan climbed on the flatbed and began tapping on the crates.

"Don't move," the officer said to Susan when she yanked her arm away. When he'd subdued her enough to get handcuffs on, he asked, "Where's the girl?"

Susan, belligerent to the core, just spat blood on the ground.

"She's in the back of the truck," Dylan said, sizing up the boxes. "The ones on top are too small. She can't fit into any of these."

He was joined by another officer.

"Help me move these," he said, trying to keep panic from building up inside him. What if she wasn't here? What if they'd already killed her?

He forced himself to breathe as he and the other officer handed cardboard boxes and wooden crates down to the people standing on the ground. He got to the bottom of the stack and slipped his fingers under the crate. The weight felt about right when he and the officer started to pick it up, but it was too small.

"Let's crack this one open," the officer said, reading Dylan's mind. "Someone hand me a crowbar!"

It took an exceedingly long time, to Dylan's mind, to pull the top off the crate. It had been secured shut with long nails that refused to give under force. His heart pounded and his mind shut down as he tried not to imagine what horrors he might find if Tammie was indeed in the box. He braced himself as he and the officer pulled the cover off the crate.

"Oh, Lord in heaven!" he cried.

Wood splintering into pieces pulled Tammie from the place she'd gone after her world went black. She didn't want to open her eyes. Her body hurt too much to move. But as fresh air surrounded her, awakening her senses, she took in a deep breath to revive herself.

She was vaguely aware of voices around her, but she didn't have the strength to move until arms wrapped under her knees and her back and lifted her out of her wooden prison.

"She has a nasty gash on her head that's bleeding pretty bad," someone said. "Are the paramedics here yet?"

She felt the rough skin of a cheek against hers and heard the voice she'd been longing to hear.

"She's alive," Dylan said, nuzzling her face and holding her close. "That's all that matters."

"Dylan?" Her voice sounded far away, even to her own ears, lost in the commotion around her.

"It's over, Tammie. I have you."

"You know, you do look a little like Keanu," she said, her eyes blinking at the bright light.

"What?"

Instead of answering, she smiled. "I'm so glad you found me."

"Me, too."

She closed her eyes and then opened them again quickly, grabbing his arm. "You're not going anywhere, are you?"

Tears were streaming down Dylan's cheeks. "Not a chance, lady. I'm not letting you out of my life. Ever."

Awareness startled her. "Susan! Dylan, she took the baby. Susan was the one who took Serena and Cash's baby. I heard them talking about it. The baby is in Colombia. Turgis has her." A tear rolled down her cheek.

"Now that we have Susan in custody, we'll be able to find Ellie. Don't you worry about that."

"How did you stop her?" Tammie said, her eyes slowly closing.

"I jumped on the truck."

Tammie's eyes flew open. "You are nuts! Do you know that, Dylan Montgomery? What is it with you and moving vehicles?"

He laughed, and it broke the tension she'd been feeling.

He'd found her. She wanted to believe that Dylan would find little Ellie, too. They had to.

"You're going to the hospital to get that head injury taken care of," Dylan said. He looked down into her eyes, and their gazes locked. "No one's going to hurt you anymore. I promise you that."

With that, she allowed herself to shut her eyes. She didn't sleep. She heard the movements of the paramedics in the ambulance, felt the warm touch of Dylan's hand holding hers. And she heard the comforting sound of his voice as he said a soft prayer of thanks to the Lord that He had answered his prayers.

EIGHTEEN

Dylan stared through the glass window into the interrogation room as the state police officer interrogated Susan. Sam Watson had already admitted to helping dig out the tunnel from the barn to the house—for a price, of course, with no questions asked and the promise of secrecy.

It hadn't taken him long to give up the information, with a little pressure from the investigation team. But after three hours of grilling, Dylan was sure Sam didn't know anything about Cash or the baby's whereabouts.

Now it was Susan's turn.

The door to the back room opened quietly. Tammie, Serena and Aurore were led into the room by another officer.

"Has she said anything yet?" Serena whispered.

"She can't hear you," the officer said. "There's no need to whisper. But if she says anything that you recognize, let us know, so we can continue asking questions in that direction."

Dylan pulled out a few chairs and motioned for them to sit. Serena, who was still a little unsteady, sat down next to Aurore.

At first, Dylan questioned whether or not it was right for Serena to be present when Susan was questioned. If

Susan revealed information about any harm that was done to Cash or little Ellie, it would be devastating for all of them, but especially for Serena.

But they all agreed that Susan's statements could touch on something that Cash might have mentioned to Serena in confidence, and that hearing something again could trigger a memory that would give them a lead to finding her family.

Tammie got up to stand next to him, all the while keeping her eyes glued to Susan, sitting on the other side of the glass.

"What were you doing there?" he heard the interrogating officer's voice say through the speaker.

"Cleaning," Susan answered, her hands folded across her chest.

"Don't get smart with me. We know you have connections with Aztec Corporation and Manuel Turgis. We know you were planted in the Davco home for some reason. What were you after? Did you find what you were looking for?"

"Yeah, clean toilets. I'm a good housekeeper."

"Things would go a whole lot easier for you if you cooperated with us. Just tell us where Cash and Ellie Montgomery are."

The officer continued grilling Susan for over four hours. Although she stubbornly held on to whatever information she had, the sag in her shoulders and her slight slouch as she sat in the chair showed that she was getting tired.

She turned directly toward the one-way mirror. Although she couldn't see them behind the glass and could only see her reflection in the mirror, anyone who'd watched enough episodes of *Law & Order* would know she was being watched.

"Look, the baby is safe," Susan finally said. "She's being well taken care of."

"Where's the baby?" the officer pressed.

She closed her eyes and sighed. "Colombia. And that's all I'm going to say."

"With who? Who has her?"

"That's all I'm going to say!"

Serena could hardly sit still in the seat.

"I'm going to take her out of here," Aurore said. "This is too much."

"No," Serena insisted.

Dylan could sympathize. It was hard enough for *him* to listen, never mind Serena. "If Susan knows where Cash and the baby are, it's best we're here to listen to any details she might give us."

Dylan turned his attention back to Susan. Tammie had been quiet, taking in everything that was being said.

The officer in the interrogation room stood up. "We can help you, if you let us. If you want protection, we can give you that. But you have to cooperate."

Her anger renewed, Susan abruptly stood up. The chair she'd been sitting in knocked over with the motion. "Don't you people get it?" she yelled. "It doesn't matter what I say or what you do. There is no protection from these people. And I'm as good as dead, just for being here. Forget about Cash Montgomery and the baby. They're gone!"

The information the police were able to get from Susan was at least enough for Sonny to do more digging in her usual way. On the drive home from the police station, Dylan relayed to his sister what little information they'd gotten regarding key people in Aztec Corporation, in the hopes that she could uncover more clues to Cash's and Ellie's whereabouts.

As soon as they got back to the mansion, Dylan pulled the portrait of Eleanor Davco and Serena off the wall and brought it down to the living room.

"The wall looks so empty now," Serena said, looking at the place where the portrait had hung for years. The days since she'd cleared her body of the drugs she'd been given had been hard, but she was thinking and talking more clearly now. While her depression over Cash and the baby was still evident in her crying bouts, she'd managed to hold herself together during the interrogation for the sake of working toward getting her family back, and had only needed to leave the room for an hour or two to rest.

"Tell me again what Byron did?" Tammie asked, brushing the dust off the top of the picture frame.

"Susan never said why she'd been planted here," Dylan said. "I'm guessing it was to find the third painting. If I'm right, this portrait is not the original painting that was done on this canvas. The stolen painting was probably given to Byron, but never delivered to its final destination. I think that's why Turgis put so much pressure on Byron."

Tammie frowned. "I don't get it. Why would Byron keep the painting? If Manuel Turgis was so upset about it, why not just give the painting to him?"

"Turgis put a lot of pressure on Byron. Perhaps he'd wanted to go straight after Eleanor became suspicious of his dealings, but Turgis wouldn't let him. We'll never know for sure. But Turgis needed Byron to continue his illegal dealings here. Without his help to launder money, his operation would stop."

"But my father continued working with Turgis," Serena said. "He gave him money. He wanted me to give him the family fortune."

"My guess is that whoever the original painting was supposed to go to put pressure on Turgis. I don't think this was ever about money. It was about power. Byron defied him by wanting to leave the organization. When Turgis refused to give him his freedom, Byron withheld the last painting, and that made Turgis lose face with his customer. He needed to make Byron pay for that. If Byron commissioned the artist to paint over the original painting with the portrait of Eleanor and Serena, this was Byron's only bargaining chip."

"It all makes sense," Aurore said. "He used to look at that painting and cry, saying it was all he had left. But what he meant was that it was all he had left to ensure his family's safety."

With the edge of a knife, Dylan pried the canvas away from the frame. "That's right. As long as Byron had the painting, they were assured some element of safety."

Aurore held the other side of the portrait. "The artist who painted this portrait died in a car accident not long after the painting was finished. There was no way at that point to find out information regarding the painting that Turgis was looking for. Byron had commissioned so many portraits from this artist that Turgis didn't know which painting was the portrait he was looking for. Only Byron knew."

As Dylan inspected the paint on the borders of the

canvas, he said, "Byron was a smart man. Turgis would have killed the entire family from the start if he'd been able to get his hands on that painting."

Tammie took a soft cloth and brushed dust off the front of the painting as she stared at the images. "Then why all those years of extorting money?"

"To ruin Byron," Aurore said. "When the statute of limitations was up on the art theft, Turgis was under bigger pressure from his buyer to get the painting back. Susan must have been planted here to find it. Only she never figured it was right under her nose the whole time. None of us did. Only Byron knew. And, of course, he must have known that if Serena had given back the painting, she was as good as dead, too. So he left that part out of his letter, hoping the family fortune would be enough to satisfy Turgis."

"And it may well be," Dylan said. "The painting was stolen a long time ago. Who knows if the original buyer is even still alive?"

He used the knife to pick at the paint on the border and then peeled a small piece back.

"What do you think?" Tammie asked.

"I can't tell for sure, but it looks as if this canvas was reused. Only a professional will be able to remove the paint and see what's underneath."

"So what do we do now?" Serena asked. "How can we use this to get Cash and Ellie back?"

Dylan dropped the knife onto the coffee table and propped the painting up against the wall. "We do what Byron was too afraid to do. We go after Turgis and dangle the painting right in front of his face."

Serena gasped. "But they'll kill Cash and Ellie!"

"We have to be realistic," he said delicately. "Susan said the baby was being taken care of. But Cash might already be dead."

Silence filled the room.

Tammie came up beside him and touched his arm. He wanted to take comfort from her, but they had to move beyond what might be to what they actually knew, to be of any good to Cash and Ellie.

Dylan cleared his throat. "The fact remains, we know where to start. If it's the last thing I do, I'm going to find Cash and Ellie. I'm going after them."

"Then I'm going, too," Tammie said resolutely.

He shook his head. "No, you're staying here. I know you all want to help with this but we have to be careful. It's much too dangerous to have all of us showing our faces on their territory."

"I can't just sit here and do nothing. This is my family, too. I want to do something," Tammie insisted.

"I know you do. And you will. We just have to be careful. But don't you worry, I have a plan. None of us are going to sit back while Cash and Ellie are left in the hands of those gangsters. I'm going after them and I'm going to make sure they don't hurt anyone in this family again."

"You mean, we're going after them," Tammie said, smiling.

He drew her into his arms and kissed her soundly on the lips. "I do like the sound of that."

All of them vowed there'd be no more secrets between them.

And later that evening, Dylan sat in the same chair he always sat in, by the window overlooking the garden in the backyard. Tammie found him there, looking intently out into the woods.

"You were right, Dylan."

He turned to her. "About what?"

She shrugged. "It's a done deal for me, too. I love you."

He smiled and opened his arms to her. She climbed into his lap as she had the other night, and was enveloped by his warm embrace. She was safe and secure. And she was in love.

"I love you, Tammie. Always."

He kissed her lightly on the lips and stroked her hair back from her face gently with his fingers.

"Do you think we'll really find them?" Tammie asked.

He kissed her head and answered honestly. "I don't know. But I'll thank the Lord every day for the rest of my life that I found you."

She closed her eyes and thought about how good that was to hear. And for the first time in a long time, Tammie finally felt that she was home.

Dear Reader,

Cradle of Secrets was such a special story for me to write not only because it's my first Steeple Hill book, but because it gave me the opportunity to delve into all those stories of prominent families and scandals that I heard growing up in a small Massachusetts town. Although Eastmeadow is fictitious, it mirrors the charm of the town I now live in.

I have always loved the sense of community that living in a small town affords, and knowing that in times of tragedy, the kindness and true strength of the human spirit prevails. The Lord is at the very core of that and I've seen His influence shine through the work of people around me many times.

Tammie and Dylan's story is one of how forgiveness and finding the truth can set you free. In writing it, I revisited many wonderful stories of neighbors helping neighbors, stories of reaching out with kindness to strangers and of how sharing faith in God can help you through the darkest of times. My wish is that all of you enjoy that same sense of community and faith surrounding you.

I hope you enjoyed Tammie and Dylan's tale. I look forward to writing many more stories of romance and suspense. I love to hear from readers, so please drop me an e-mail at LisaMondello@aol.com and I'll let you know about my latest news and what future stories I have in the works.

Many blessings,
Lisa Mondello

QUESTIONS FOR DISCUSSION

1. Aaron and Connie Gardner had to make a split-second decision that changed the course of their lives forever. Have you ever made a tough decision that changed your life? What was it?

2. Tammie struggles with forgiving her parents throughout the story. How did she rely on her faith to help her through her healing and forgiveness?

3. People handle stress differently. With the tragedy that Tammie endured, she felt herself pulling away from the Lord instead of reaching to Him for support. Who or what made her realize how far she'd pulled away? How did she find her way back again?

4. Dylan feels a heavy weight of responsibility toward his brother which is normal for the eldest child in a family. When something happens to a sibling, it's easy to blame yourself for not doing enough to protect them. Has this ever happened in your family and what did you do to help you through that guilt?

5. When the story opens, Tammie's faith is shattered when she learns the people who raised her weren't her biological parents. She feels hurt and betrayed. Has anyone you loved and trusted ever betrayed you, even if it was for a good reason? How did you deal with it?

6. Dylan grapples with his anger toward Serena and blames her for his brother, Cash, disappearing. How does he come to realize that Serena is as much a victim as Cash is? How do his feelings toward Serena change as he uncovers the truth?

7. A secret can rear its ugly head if it is left to fester too long. In this story the truth sets many of the characters free. Do you think Aurore and Trudie should have told the truth long before they did? Would it have made a difference for Serena and Tammie if they'd known the truth earlier?

8. Friendships often grow into romantic relationships. What stopped Tammie from pursuing a romantic relationship with Bill and what is it about Dylan that drew her to him so quickly and helped bring about their romantic relationship?

9. Byron Davco made a mistake in connecting himself with the Aztec Corporation and let greed color his judgment. What pushed him to ignore right from wrong and engage in illegal activity that ultimately hurt his family?

10. Dylan's belief in his brother's innocence is noble. Have you ever believed in someone despite the outward appearance of their guilt? How did it change you and your relationship with that person?

INTRODUCING

Love Inspired.

HISTORICAL

A NEW TWO-BOOK SERIES.

Every month, acclaimed
inspirational authors
will bring you engaging stories
rich with romance, adventure
and faith set in a variety
of vivid historical times.

History begins on **February 12**
wherever you buy books.

Steeple
Hill®

www.SteepleHill.com

REQUEST YOUR FREE BOOKS!
2 FREE RIVETING INSPIRATIONAL NOVELS
PLUS 2 FREE MYSTERY GIFTS

Love Inspired®
SUSPENSE

YES! Please send me 2 FREE Love Inspired® Suspense novels and my 2 FREE mystery gifts. After receiving them, if I don't wish to receive any more books, I can return the shipping statement marked "cancel." If I don't cancel, I will receive 4 brand-new novels every month and be billed just $3.99 per book in the U.S. or $4.74 per book in Canada, plus 25¢ shipping and handling per book and applicable taxes, if any*. That's a savings of 20% off the cover price! I understand that accepting the 2 free books and gifts places me under no obligation to buy anything. I can always return a shipment and cancel at any time. Even if I never buy another book from Steeple Hill, the two free books and gifts are mine to keep forever.

123 IDN EL5H 323 IDN ELQH

Name _____ (PLEASE PRINT)

Address _____ Apt. #

City _____ State/Prov. _____ Zip/Postal Code

Signature (if under 18, a parent or guardian must sign)

Order online at www.LoveInspiredSuspense.com

Or mail to Steeple Hill Reader Service™:

IN U.S.A.: P.O. Box 1867, Buffalo, NY 14240-1867
IN CANADA: P.O. Box 609, Fort Erie, Ontario L2A 5X3

Not valid to current Love Inspired Suspense subscribers.

Want to try two free books from another series?
Call 1-800-873-8635 or visit www.morefreebooks.com

* Terms and prices subject to change without notice. NY residents add applicable sales tax. Canadian residents will be charged applicable provincial taxes and GST. This offer is limited to one order per household. All orders subject to approval. Credit or debit balances in a customer's account(s) may be offset by any other outstanding balance owed by or to the customer. Please allow 4 to 6 weeks for delivery.

Your Privacy: Steeple Hill is committed to protecting your privacy. Our Privacy Policy is available online at www.eHarlequin.com or upon request from the Reader Service. From time to time we make our lists of customers available to reputable firms who may have a product or service of interest to you. If you would prefer we not share your name and address, please check here. ☐

LISUS07

Love Inspired.
SUSPENSE

TITLES AVAILABLE NEXT MONTH

Don't miss these four stories in December

HER CHRISTMAS PROTECTOR by Terri Reed

Running from her abusive ex-husband, Faith Delange found shelter in Sisters, Oregon. But how secure was her haven? The longer she stayed, the more she endangered her new friends, including protective rancher Luke Campbell.

BURIED SINS by Marta Perry
The Three Sisters Inn

Caroline Hampton feared her husband was involved in something shady, but he died before she could confront him...didn't he? A string of dangerous incidents implied otherwise. Caroline fled to her sisters' inn, but trouble—and the suspicions of Police Chief Zachary Burkhalter—followed her home....

HARD EVIDENCE by Roxanne Rustand
Snow Canyon Ranch

Human remains were found behind the isolated cabins Janna McAllister was fixing up on her family ranch. And she suspected someone lurked out there even still. Her unexpected lodger, Deputy Sheriff Michael Robertson, made the single mother feel safe. Until she unwittingly tempted a killer out of the woodwork.

BLUEGRASS PERIL by Virginia Smith

When her boss was murdered, the police suspected single mom Becky Dennison. To clear her name, Becky teamed up with Scott Lewis, from a neighboring breeder's farm, to find the truth. In this Kentucky race, the stakes were life or death.

LISCNM1107